About This Village

About This Village

Peter Douglas

THE BOYDELL PRESS

Author's Note

All characters in this book are imaginary, and bear no resemblance to living persons.

Published by The Boydell Press
an imprint of Boydell & Brewer Ltd
PO Box 9, Woodbridge, Suffolk IP12 3DF

ISBN 0-85115 133 7

Printed and bound in Great Britain by
Redwood Burn Limited
Trowbridge & Esher

About This Village

About This Volume

CHAPTER ONE

A TASTE OF COUNTRY LIFE.

Running a small village General Store and Post Office in the depths of the Norfolk countryside was hard work, especially to two city types such as myself, and Maggie, my wife. There were many compensations, though, and we had long ago decided that this was the way of life for us. Whenever we listened to the radio, or read a newspaper, or heard of the crime, the vandalism, the strikes, and the other troubles that seemed at times to beset the whole country, and then looked out of our cottage windows, at the peaceful village, the thatched roofs, the windmill, the water, and the birds, we counted our blessings, and said a prayer of thanks that we had taken the plunge and left the city, and settled down in a remote village that was so small that it was very seldom shown on any map. When troubles seemed to be brewing everywhere, there was quite a lot to be said for living in the middle of nowhere.

We earned far less money than we had done in the

city, but we led a life that was far, far richer. We knew contentment, and valued it. We had our problems, of course, but they were small, human ones, and on a scale that we could cope with. Apart from the slower, more old-fashioned way of life, there were the characters of the village. They were regarded by us as an unexpected bonus, and in our new position, right in the very heart of the village, we had the opportunity to observe them, as they went about their lives and businesses.

They were such individuals, each one unique, and yet like members of the same family, each sharing the same admirable characteristics, such as self-reliance, basic honesty, and a great sense of loyalty to their village community. They kept us fascinated, from the younger ones, such as Whistling Jack, the local builder, and his muscular but clumsy labourer John, to the pensioners, such as Ben, John's father, with his permanently ragged appearance, and Percy, the ex-infantryman, with his neat and dapper turnout. One of our greatest pleasures, after working such regular hours for some time, was to make a break in our own routine, and for a short time, join in theirs. Such was our intention when we decided to close the shop early, one Saturday afternoon.

I felt cheerful as I watched the clock slowly counting off the minutes. Normally we stayed open until six o'clock on Saturdays, but today was different. We were going to close at lunchtime, for today was the day when the village held its annual vegetable and flower show in the village hall. Even if we had stayed open, we would have had no trade to speak of, as almost everyone in the village would be at the show. Maggie and I intended to be there, too.

I was looking forward to seeing the display of locally grown vegetables, and perhaps learning a thing or two from the growers. With the large garden that went with the business, I was forced to take some interest in gardening, but though I found vegetable growing a pleasant and relaxing pastime, I could never produce results that would stand comparison with the locals. Maggie had remarked that if they stood at their back doors and flung the seeds across the garden in handfuls, they would still probably achieve better results than I did, in spite of all the care that I took. I had to agree with her.

I was finishing off the last of the paperwork in the Post Office when the phone rang. It was a telegram, for me to deliver. I looked at the clock again, for the hundredth time. It was about half a minute to twelve. Another few seconds and we would have stopped taking telegrams for the day. After twelve on Saturdays, all telegrams were delivered by motor bike, from the city, until nine on Monday morning.

"Just my luck," I said to Maggie. "I only hope that it isn't a message for some farmer, way out in the wilds." It wasn't. It was for Granny Coster, an eccentric old widow who lived at the other end of the village street. "I think I'll get changed and have a bite to eat now," I said. "Then I'll be all ready for the show, when we close up at one. I can take the 'gram then; it's nothing important, just a line or two telling Granny to expect some visitor over the weekend. You can be getting ready while I take it, then we'll be at the show for two o'clock, easily." "You'd better not be late," said Maggie. "You promised Miss Money that you'd be there on time, and no-one ever breaks a promise to Miss Money."

"Oh, it's 'im," said Granny to no-one in particular, when I appeared at her open cottage door. "Come you on in then." She flapped a grubby tea towel at a cat that was sitting in the middle of the table. The cat ambled slowly to the edge, and jumped off, onto the draining board. Granny picked up a cracked mug, and wiped it on a greyish coloured garment that was hanging on a clothes horse, amidst a tangle of anonymous bits of feminine apparel. I stole a closer look at the garment, and my suspicions were confirmed. The garment that she had used was in fact a large pair of very old-fashioned knickers.

"'Ave a cup o' tea, will yer?" asked Granny. I hastily assured the old lady that I had just had several cups, before I left the Post Office. I looked round the cottage. The old lady had been baking. In the hearth there were three crusty loaves, half lifted from their tins, slowly cooling. The little dog, that had left off digging in the hedgerow to greet me, sniffed at the bread, and then licked tentatively at one loaf. I was speechless for a moment, and handed the telegram dumbly to Granny. "Oh yes. Thank 'ee," she said, and placed it on the mantel-shelf without bothering to open it. "They'll be coming this Sunday," she said. "I did know it, all along, you know, but they keep having to remind me." She scratched her head with a grimy hand. "I keeps forgettin' things lately," she cackled. "Yes, I understand," I said, and gave her what I hoped was a kindly smile.

Granny waved away a couple of flies that were crawling round the top of the milk bottle, and poured some of the milk into the mug. The little dog sniffed around the floor, examining the debris there, evidently finding a couple of edible morsels in his search. Two cats watched the dog sleepily, one on the draining board, the other one now in the middle of the table.

"I really must be going now." I said. "They're expecting me at the show this afternoon, you know." I edged towards the door. "Why, I'll be goin along there meself in a minute or two," said Granny. "Here, you finish off this mug o' tea, while I goes and gets me hat. Then I can go along with you. I likes a bit o' company." She thrust the mug into my hand, and went into the front room. In her absence I quickly tipped the contents of the mug down the sink, watched accusingly by the little dog and the two cats, and then stood holding the mug, and trying to smile.

When Granny reappeared, she was wearing an enormous black hat with a huge overhanging brim. The hat was festooned with at least half a dozen hatpins that were sticking out at such painful angles that they gave me quite a turn when I first saw them. Then I realised that they must all have been badly bent, otherwise they would have penetrated the old lady's brain. She was also wearing a long coat of the same dusty black, and it reached down to her ankles.

"Well then, how do I look?" she cackled. I looked at the sooty fingermarks on her forehead, where she had scraped her hair back, and at the old food stains down the front of the coat, and at the cracks in her old black shoes. "As nice as ever, Granny," I said. The frail old lady cackled again, and then astounded me as she grasped my arm with a grip like iron. "Let's be a-goin then," she said. "It's many a long year since a man walked me down the village street. I'll bet this will set some of 'em talkin." We left, Granny cackling now and again, and the dog and the cats watching us through the kitchen window.

It was a very long and slow journey back to the Post Office, with Granny hanging on my arm. It wasn't that the old lady was heavy, in fact she weighed no more than a child, but she did tend to lean on me, and drag her feet rather a lot. And she had a will of her own.

I happened to catch sight of our reflections in a cottage window as we went along, and the sudden sight of this staggering stranger with the peculiar gait, and the dark and sinister figure, that could easily have been a vampire bat, clinging to his side, so alarmed me that I tried to increase our speed slightly. Granny wasn't having any of that. She didn't say anything by way of protest, but she paused for a moment to admire a garden, then

11

after that went slower than ever. Every time I tried to increase the pace. her dragging foot caught my ankle, right on the bone, and I slowed down again.

One of the organisers of the show, and any other social function in the village, was Miss Money, and immaculate as ever in large flowery hat and white gloves, she overtook us as we trudged along. She was obviously on her way to the village hall, and she waved one white gloved hand to us as she passed. Then she seemed to be overcome by a sudden fit of coughing, and she went hurrying on ahead of us, her face hidden in her handkerchief.

Arriving eventually at the Post Office, I rapped on the shop door. Maggie appeared, and looked at us in surprise, but opened up without comment. I ushered my elderly companion into the shop, and prising her grip free, brought the Post Office stool round the counter, so that she could sit while we waited for Maggie. The old lady sagged on the stool for all the world like some great black bird perching, and I went to put a plaster on my ankle, where Granny's dragging foot had taken the skin off.

"I'm ready," said Maggie, and I turned towards Granny. She had left her stool and was bent over the provision counter, staring into the refrigerated display. Maggie kept this piece of equipment so spotlessly clean that I would have prepared to undergo major surgery in its gleaming white depths. Granny looked at the boiled ham and corned beef with deep distrust. "I can't never see how folk can bear to buy that sort of stuff off you," she said. "Once a ham has been cut into, all sorts of germs can get in. Same with corned beef and all that stuff. I'm very particular about things like that, you know. I wouldn't risk it. I always buys a pork pie. They're wrapped up, so you know that they're still clean."

"Er, if you'd like to go on ahead with Granny," I said

to Maggie, "I'll lock up and follow you." "Oh, that's all right," said Maggie, with an unusually bright smile, "You two carry on. I can lock up by myself." I was about to reason with her, but Granny's frail hand gripped my arm again, with staggering strength. "Come you on," she said, steering me towards the door. "We don't want to miss anything."

We set off along the village street again, at the same painfully slow pace. I did look back a time or two, surprised that Maggie didn't catch up with us, but she also seemed to be walking very slowly. One time she seemed to have stopped because she had got something in her eye, and another time she was just sort of leaning weakly against a garden fence, holding her sides, as if she had a stitch and was trying to get her breath back.

Once inside the village hall, I aimed Granny towards the refreshment stall, and then at last made my escape. I had a ready-made excuse for leaving the old dear, for I had been gently press-ganged, by the delightful Miss Money, into running a craft stall for the afternoon. After working all week long in the Post Office, the very last thing in the world that I wanted to do was to stand behind a counter for someone else, but as all these occasions were supported so well by everyone else in the village, and so much money was raised for so many good causes, I felt that I simply could not refuse.

The stall was piled high with home-made goods and craft work. There were items of turned wood and carved wood, pottery and corn dollies, hand woven ties and shawls. The show had been well advertised, and crowds from the surrounding villages had turned up. I was soon busy, and the stall, which I had assumed would be either amusing or boring, suddenly began to look very much like work. After a while I began to have difficulty keeping the stall filled up, as eager hands grabbed the goods and proffered money. Perhaps the volume of trade was connected with the low prices being charged, or maybe a shortage of goods of that particular type, but whatever the reason, I was soon working flat out. If any article had lost its price ticket, a hasty guess, on the low side, was all that I could manage.

While I was working so hard, Maggie was having an enjoyable time. She had been asked to judge the pickles and preserves, and as they came much later, after all the vegetable prizes had been awarded, she took the opportunity to wander around the show, and bring me running reports on any interesting happenings. She turned up once with her camera, ready to take a picture of the colourful stall. Finding her view obscured, she put the camera down for a moment, while she served a couple of customers who were in the way, and that was the last that she saw of it. Miss Money, thinking that she was doing me a good turn, stopped on her way past and sold the camera to a delighted housewife for less than the cost of the film that was in it. I tried very hard to get my revenge by selling her hat, which she had taken off and placed at the back of the stall, but everyone that I offered it to recognised it at once as being Miss Money's hat. The large flowery hats, like the white gloves, were part of Miss Money's image.

When the judging was about to start, Miss Money left, taking Maggie with her. I realised after they had gone, that I was very thirsty. I hadn't had a drink of any kind with my hurried snack, and had been repulsed by Granny's proffered beverage. I would just have to go thirsty now. The refreshment stall wasn't all that far away, but I was on my own, and the customers kept coming.

The vegetable prizes were to be awarded by Lady Blanche, who lived at the Hall, which was on the outskirts of the village. Every village seemed to have its titled resident, and Lady Blanche was ours. She made

14

her way almost regally around the village hall, accompanied by Miss Money and the vicar. Their first stop was at the marrows.

Many of the gardeners of the village specialised in marrows. I never cared for them myself, and Maggie wasn't too keen on them either, so I never made any attempt to grow them, which was just as well, for had I done so, I doubt whether I would have been able to produce anything like the giants that were regarded as being of normal size by the villagers. Even if I had by chance been able to match their success, a terrible fate might have befallen me. I might have become infected by the strange disease that caused such rivalries and jealousies, and that seemed to affect all the growers of marrows.

This rivalry seemed to grow in direct proportion to the size of the marrows themselves. The closest of friends, and even families, had been known to fall out over the things, and secret recipes for the feeding of the monsters were handed down from father to son, and never let out of the family. If only half the rumours that Maggie and I had heard about these recipes were true, then it was a wonder that the things were fit for human consumption at all.

The story of Hubby's marrows was well known in the district. In the previous year, Hubby had grown some of the biggest marrows that had ever been seen in the village. At the annual show, however, Hubby had been conspicuous by his absence. Gardeners who had decided not to show their produce after hearing of Hubby's giants were incensed when the prizes were awarded to specimens that would have been easily beaten by the marrows that they had left at home. The reason why Hubby had not shown his marrows soon leaked out. Only a few of his relatives and closest friends were allowed to see the actual marrows, and the vicar was refused permission to even peep at them, as were the many women who showed interest.

The reason for all this shyness, so the story went, was that someone had got at the vegetables when they were small, and had scratched them with a penknife, or something similar. As the marrows grew, so did the scars that they carried, and when they came to full size, they each bore, in huge letters along their sides, a very rude remark indeed.

Hubby had vowed that he would discover the saboteur, and have his revenge. During the following twelve months, the locals forgot all about the incident, but Hubby did not, and in the fullness of time, his chance came.

Young 'Enry, who was one of the local farmers, and not all that young, in spite of the nickname, had some enormous marrows entered in this year's show. They were the talk of the village, and it had been assumed for some time that he would walk off with first prize. The kitchen garden of 'Enry's farm was justly famous for its produce, and no doubt 'Enry's connection with racehorses had something to do with this. There were only three marrows set out on the table this year, and the other two together wouldn't have weighed much more than Hubby's massive exhibit. Lady Blanche stared at the marrow, and her eyes widened. "Just look at this one." she said to the vicar. "Isn't it absolutely perfect?" The vicar agreed, and lifted the monster gently from its resting place, feeling the weight of it in his hands. He turned it over as he did so, and Lady Blanche tut-tutted, and shook her head. "It's marked," she said. "What a terrible shame! What a tragedy! Oh dear, Oh, dear." The vicar looked, and saw the marks. They were upside down to him, but Miss Money, her face showing her concern, turned her head on one side and read out the words that scarred the other side of the marrow. "AND YOU TOO," she said, and then looked from the vicar to Lady Blanche with a puzzled expression.

"I'm afraid," said Lady Blanche, "that although this is a magnificent specimen, it doesn't qualify for first prize. It's very sad, but size alone is not enough, the marrow has to be as nearly as possible perfect. This impressive entry must be third." She gave the other two smaller entries a cursory examination, and placed the winners ticket in front of one of them. "This one is the winner," she said. "It's not as big, but it is nearer to being perfect." There was an outburst of angry muttering from the crowd. "T'ain't fair," said one disgruntled gardener loudly, "Specially after what happened last year, when all the titchy little things won all the prizes." 'Enry looked at the winning marrow, which he knew had been submitted by Hubby, and ground his teeth noisily. "What kind of a show is this?" he said to the crowd. "The prizes are going to the worst stuff again. That there marrow ain't worth cutting. You'll find better than that in almost any garden in the village." There was a chorus of agreement, and Miss Money gasped, and raised her white gloved hand to her flushed cheek. Lady Blanche must have heard the remarks, but didn't condescend to reply. She passed on calmly to the next stall, leaving 'Enry gripping the edge of the table in frustration. There wasn't a great deal that one could do in his situation, when the judge was an extremely dignified female, old enough to be his mother, and titled to boot. He looked at the coveted winners card, resting in front of a marrow that in boxing terms wouldn't even have been in the light heavyweight class, and his neck turned a deep red. "It's a darn good job that she's a Lady," he told the crowd, "and that I'm a gentleman."

17

On the next table, several bunches of carrots were arranged. They were all very good carrots indeed, but one bunch was almost half as big again as their nearest rivals. They were a good shape, a good colour, and they looked delicious. Lady Blanche, anxious to improve the atmosphere if she could, raised her voice slightly as she spoke to the vicar. "These are beautiful specimens," she said, and the crowd agreed in whispers amongst themselves. She picked up one of the biggest carrots, and turned it over in her hand. As she did so, her smile faded. "What on earth are these?" she said. "There are large holes all over this one." She handed him the carrot, and after looking at it closely, the vicar examined the rest of the bunch. They were all the same. "Oh dear me," he said. "What could have caused all those, do you think, wireworm?" "Carrot fly, perhaps," said Miss Money, trying to show that she did know at least a little about gardening.

"Oh that's not a disease or anything," said Whistling Jack, the village's jobbing builder, from the crowd. "Them carrots are mine, and it wasn't a worm or a fly that made them holes, it was me." Lady Blanche turned to him and shook her head sadly. "You do know that you've just broken one of the major rules, don't you?" she said. "The judges are not supposed to know the identity of the entrants until after all the prizes have been awarded." "Well it don't make any difference in this case, does it?" said Jack. "There ain't any competition, so the first prize must be mine."

"Why did you want to make all these holes in your lovely carrots?" Miss Money asked. Jack grinned. "I didn't want to," he said. "It just sort of happened." "How?" persisted Miss Money. "Well," said Jack. "You know how most vegetable plots around here have wire netting around 'em, to keep the rabbits out? Well my plot's like that, except for one hole. I always leave a small gap, so as if any rabbit wants to get in there, he can. Now, if I think that there's one in there, I wait by the hole, with the old air gun. I only have one shot in the gun, so that the rabbit always gets a fair chance, and I do miss some of 'em. But I get one or two as well." He grinned, and winked at the judge knowingly. "It's surprising how many meat dinners a fellow can get out of a well planned vegetable patch," he said.

The crowd quietly applauded Jack's explanation, but Lady Blanche looked sadder than ever. "So all these holes were actually caused by you, shooting the carrots by mistake?" she said. "Yes," said Jack, "But it doesn't matter a bit, 'cos they're not diseased, and they're the biggest carrots for miles around." Lady Blanche sighed. "Once again, I'm sorry," she said, "but these large carrots are not perfect specimens, they're damaged. The first prize must go to these carrots here." She placed the card in front of another entry, and the crowd gasped, and then began to rumble with dissent. Jack looked at the puny winners with contempt. "Why, most folk give better stuff than that to their in-laws," he stated loudly. The crowd agreed with him. "You should have used some of the biggest ones, to plug up the holes in yours." said another disgruntled gardener. The vicar tried to smile at this, and Miss Money went pink with embarrassment again. Lady Blanche merely looked sad, and moved on to the next stall.

Miss Money, perhaps a little more sensitive than most people, was becoming more and more concerned by the way that the crowd was muttering and grumbling as the prizes were being awarded. "You know, this sort of thing would never have happened if Percy had been showing his produce. He would have won every prize, and everyone would have agreed that he deserved to win," she said. The vicar stopped and looked round. "Isn't he here?" he asked. "The best gardener in the whole village,

19

and not exhibiting?" "I think that I can explain his absence," said Miss Money.

The story of Percy's garden had spread throughout the village, but obviously hadn't come to the ears of the vicar. The trouble had all started with Percy's neighbour, John.

When John had first bought his homing pigeons, Percy had been enraged. His gardener's instinct made him dislike all pigeons, and as his garden adjoined that of the cottage where John and his father Ben lived, Percy could foresee all kinds of trouble. When approached on the subject, John had been far from helpful. He said that he intended to keep his pigeons so well fed that they wouldn't need to pillage anyone's garden, and in any case, it was a free country. John's father, Ben, who was a pensioner, like Percy, and one of his closest friends, couldn't help. "If you tell him not to do a thing, he'll most likely go ahead and do it, just to be awkward," he said. "He's not a boy any more, he's a grown man." "Har," said Percy. "He might have grown, and I'll admit that he's big enough, but he's got a long way to go yet." Percy cornered John in the bar of the village pub, and warned the youngster that he might be heading for trouble. He muttered darkly that anyone could mistake a homing pigeon for a wood pigeon, and as they all tasted very much alike, John's birds would very likely all end up in the pot, in a very short time.

Percy appeared to be right, for as soon as John had owned his birds long enough to allow them to fly freely, they began to disappear, one by one. John checked to see whether they had flown back to their previous home, but they had not, and after a few weeks, his loft was bare. The last of his homing pigeons had gone.

John was bitter about the loss of his birds, but for most of the time he remained silent and brooding. On one occasion, in the village pub, he did have an outburst in which he flatly accused Percy of murdering his feathered friends, but mostly he kept his thoughts to himself, and just brooded.

Maggie and I were in the habit of taking a stroll on most fine evenings, after we had closed the shop and had tea. We would usually arrive home at dusk, and often, as we made our way back, we would catch sight of John in the distance, at the bottom of his garden. He would be crouched against the fence, and holding a large can, or bucket. At regular intervals he would dip his hand into the container, and fling something into the air. Whatever it was that he threw, we could never make out in the dusk, and his manner was so furtive that we never called out to him, but walked by quickly, as though we hadn't seen him. Whatever it was that he was throwing though, it was always carried away from us by the prevailing wind, and over Percy's garden.

When the warmer weather came, and weeding was in full swing, Percy began to show signs of distress. His garden, which had always been known as the best kept in the whole village, became a mass of tiny weed seedlings. He had every type of weed imaginable, and even a couple that he had never seen, in all his years as a gardener. As fast as he pulled them out they sprang up again. He hoed where he could, and pulled by hand where he couldn't, but he was fighting a losing battle. After spending a large amount of money on sprays, and still not winning, his spirits began to flag.

"It's just like trying to keep mice out of a haystack." he told the company in the bar of the village pub. "As fast as I do one in, another two spring up in their places. I've been so busy with it all that I haven't even had time to think about the show this year."

John, who was not noted for his soft heart, appeared to sympathise with the old man. He said, in a somewhat clumsy fashion, that he thought that nature had a balance, and that Percy, probably in all innocence, had probably upset that balance. "You can't ever fight nature and win, you know." he said, speaking to the old pensioner as though he was years his junior. "You know, I'd like to bet, Percy, that if you'd had a few more birds, say the odd couple of pigeons, a-flying round your plot, all this here trouble of yours might never have happened."

It was Percy's turn to go quiet and thoughtful after that. He seemed for a time to be brooding in much the same way that John had done. John, having at last broken his silence, was now chatting away normally with the other locals. Percy did keep sneaking the odd sideways glance at him, and his looks, at first full of anger, gradually changed, until they eventually held a certain amount of respect that he had never shown John before.

Miss Money had just finished explaining Percy's absence to the vicar when the old man himself showed up. He walked smartly into the hall, and then stopped dead in his tracks as he looked round in astonishment at the exhibits that had been awarded first prizes. "Gaw, bless me," he said. "If I'd only known, I could have won, after all. This lot here is a load of old rubbish, I throw things away that are better than some of this stuff. What's going on then?" The vicar went over to him quickly. Enough had been said about the prizewinners, he thought, and it would be best if he could change the subject. "Ah, Percy," he said warmly. "I hear that you're not doing your usual amount of gardening this year." Percy looked at him sourly, and then his gaze went back to the prizewinners again. "You've always told me that you were far too busy in your garden on Sundays to come to church." said the vicar. "But surely that can't apply this year. Tell me, when might I expect to see you at one of my services?" It was not the best of times to ask the old man that particular question. He shook his head at the exhibits, and then answered. "You can expect to see me when greenflies is killed by prayin', not sprayin'," he snapped, and stomped grumpily away.

While tempers were becoming frayed in the vegetable section, my craft stall was doing a booming trade in its corner. The till was full of notes, and certain items of stock were getting short. Old Charlie, one of the village's oldest pensioners, came towards me through the crowd, walking slowly and carrying two mugs of tea. "Your missus asked me to bring you one o' these." he said. "And I'll just sit down at your stall and have mine with you, if you don't mind." I took the tea from him, and put it down as another customer came up. "That vegetable section is like a madhouse," said Charlie, sitting down on a box at the back of the stall, his head on a level with the goods. I served the customer, and then there came a slight lull. I turned and sat down with relief, facing the old man. "Thanks, Charlie," I said, and took up the tea.

As I sipped, I watched Old Charlie. He looked somehow different, but I couldn't think why. At last I had to say something. "What's happened to your face, Charlie?" I said. "You look odd, if you don't mind me saying so." "I've taken my top teeth out," said Charlie. "I've been tasting a bit of your wife's raspberry jam, and the pips have got under my plate; that's why I'm sitting here, out of sight for a bit. I've stuck 'em in my tea, you see, to give 'em a bit of a soak." I had to hide a smile, at the thought of the old man washing his false teeth in his tea. Charlie took up his mug and stuck a grubby finger into it. Then he wiped the smile from my face very quickly. "Here," he said, "My teeth ain't here. This ain't my mug o' tea at all. You must be drinking mine."

By about five o'clock the stock had almost all gone, and so had the customers. I started packing up the stall. The vegetable prizes had all been awarded, and I wanted to go and find Maggie, and watch her tasting and judging the preserves. I didn't envy her task, as some of the recipes for chutney that were used by the housewives of the village were most certainly acquired tastes. One local farmer swore that his wife's chutney had not only caused his teeth to work loose and fall out, but that it had also had the very same effect on the false ones that he had got to replace them.

Miss Money came over to my stall, and complimented me on the sale of so much stock. Together we counted the takings, watched by other members of the Village Hall Committee. As we counted, it became clear to me that I had earned almost as much money, in running the stall for just the one afternoon, as I did in a long hard week in the Post Office. The committee were also agreeably surprised at the size of the takings, but they all seemed to be looking at me in a very peculiar way. It was blunt old Charlie who eventually summed up their feelings. "Gaw," he said, "You must be the richest man in the whole blarsted village, and for miles around. If you can make that amount o' money, and in that bit o' time, what must you be making in a full week in that shop o' yours?" The others nodded their agreement, and looked at me as though they had caught me stealing the bread out of the mouths of little children.

In vain I pointed out the difference between turnover and profit. I added that whereas I had run the stall single-handed, in the shop I had to pay the wages of an assistant. I told them how low the profit margin on general foodstuffs was, compared with giftware and fancy goods. I said that the shop had overheads and expenses that the stall did not. I was wasting my breath. They remained unconvinced, and I handed the takings over to Miss Money in a gloomy mood.

Then I had an idea. I reached under the stall, and dragged out the hamper that Maggie and I had donated as first prize in the raffle. We always gave a hamper, whatever the occasion, and people now expected it of us. We had been extra generous in the making up of this one, and had even added a bottle of wine, as a touch of class.

"How's that?" I said proudly, flinging back the lid and displaying the carefully arranged contents. There was a long silence, broken at last by an eloquent sniff from Old Charlie.

As I pushed my way through the crowd towards the table where Maggie was performing her duties, I couldn't help but overhear the conversation of the crowd. "I only hope that the judging of the chutney is going to be a bit fairer than the judging of the vegetables was." said the disgruntled gardener, as he and his wife watched Maggie keenly as she moved slowly along the row of jars, tasting a minute sample from each one. "It had better be," said his wife. "My chutney takes some beating, and if I don't win, then I'll want the recipe of the one that does." I closed my eyes as I listened, and said a silent prayer as Maggie prepared to make her choice. "Please let her award the prize to some well-liked local housewife." I prayed. "Some motherly type, with rosy cheeks and spotless apron. A woman with a cheerful smile and a reputation for good wholesome cooking. The kind of person no-one will be able to argue about."

As we waited, Miss Money, who was standing on a chair in the corner, was calling out the numbers of the winning raffle tickets, and people were searching through their pockets as the numbers of the third prize, and then the second, were announced. When the number of the winner of the first prize was called, no-one claimed the prize, but most people, realising that they hadn't won, threw their tickets to the floor in disgust, then concentrated on the judging. Miss Money came hurrying across the floor, waving to me. "You've won first prize," she called, over the heads of the crowd. "You've won your own hamper back again." I wished then with all my heart that I hadn't bought any raffle tickets, but simply given Miss Money the price of half a dozen. I glanced round at the crowd. It had been the members of the Village Hall Committee who had looked upon me with disfavour only a short time ago, and that had been unpleasant. Now it was the whole crowd, and it was unbearable. They turned as one man, and looked at me with something that was very close to hostility. "First the vegetable prizes, and now this," said the gardener, loudly. "Who's going to win the chutney prize then, the vicar's wife?"

"Er, raffle it again," I called to Miss Money, loudly, so that the crowd would hear. "Draw another ticket, and let someone else win it." "Oh, thank you, that's very generous indeed." the lady smiled. "What the devil did you expect him to say?" said an anonymous voice. "He's got a ruddy shop full of that stuff, ain't he?"

Miss Money called out another number, while Maggie closed her eyes and made her final tasting. The people in the crowd began searching on the floor, looking for their abandoned tickets.

It is a simple fact that fifty people, all bending down together, will not fit into the same space that was adequate to accommodate the same fifty people, standing up. Heads were banged together, and tempers snapped like dry twigs. It wasn't only heads that banged either. If two people, standing back to back, suddenly bent down, the same thing happened to their other ends, and there was so much pushing and shoving that the row of jars on Maggie's table began to rock dangerously. Percy was standing in the crowd, innocently discussing vegetable growing with a farmer's wife, when the lady behind him suddenly bent down. This movement gave Percy such a violent shove in the rear that he had no choice but to grab the farmers wife as he lurched towards her

26

and propel her backwards through the swing doors at
high speed. Her husband, who was already in an irritable
mood because his crooked parsnips had been passed
over by the judges, saw the effect of this movement, but
not the cause. He pushed his way through the crowd,
in the direction of his disappearing spouse, his nostrils
flaring as he went.

The opening of the door by Percy admitted a strong

27

draught, and the raffle tickets fluttered around the floor like autumn leaves. When the vicar slipped and fell flat on his back while trying to avoid being crushed to the bosom of a wizened spinster, he got no sympathy at all from the rest of the crowd. "Get up and out of the way," snarled a housewife at him. "You're lying on my ticket and it might be the winner."

"It's here," shouted the disgruntled gardener, and his wife waved the winning ticket aloft. "We've won," she crowed, and for the very first since I had noticed the man, he was actually smiling. His wife too seemed to be a different woman as they went and collected their hamper. Perhaps now the rude comments would cease, and the crowd would adopt a more friendly attitude towards the judges. "Come on, Maggie," I prayed. "Make a good choice, now that they're in a better mood."

Maggie made her decision. She went back along the row of jars and placed the winner's ticket in front of one that was labelled, in a very shaky hand, "CHUTNIE." Then she took another tiny bit on her spoon, and tasted it with obvious pleasure. "It really has got something different, something unique about it." she said. "Here, try a bit." I took the offered sample. "It's unusual." I agreed, trying to think what it was that the taste reminded me of. The vicar took up a spoon, and helped himself to a portion. He nodded his approval of the choice. "It's certainly got something different about it." he said. The housewives in the crowd, hiding their disappointment, gathered around the table, demanding a taste of the superior product.

We were all standing around Maggie, with spoons in our hands, commenting favourably, and smacking our lips, when the winner herself came pushing her way through the crowd. "I'm glad you all like it." she called. "I'll give the recipe to anyone who wants it, if I can remember it right. Do you know, I've been making that-stuff for over thirty years, and this is the first time that I've ever won anything with it. I wonder why that is?" We all stopped smacking our lips, and turned to the speaker. Maggie stared at the jar of chutney, now at least half empty. "Oh heavens," said the vicar, and dropped his spoon with a clatter. Miss Money looked for one moment as if she was about to spit her chutney out onto the floor, then she remembered that she was a lady, and with great courage she gulped it down, and then covered her mouth with her handkerchief. The crowd of housewives turned and gave Maggie a series of murderous looks, upon which she turned pale and sat down suddenly. "Oh, no," she said, staring at the winner. "It's Granny Coster."

CHAPTER TWO.

THE BELLS, THE BELLS.

To anyone living and working in the city, as Maggie and I had done, and feeling at times discontented with their way of life, the idea of living in some remote village is bound to be attractive at times. The rural grass is always greener. For anyone who actually takes the plunge and makes the change, and goes to live deep in the countryside, there are many surprises in store, for the realities of such a way of life are so very different from the expectations. Life did move at a slower pace of course, but things didn't always run smoothly, and when some plan failed to produce the expected result, or some pet scheme went wrong, then the reaction was pretty much the same as it would have been in city life, but there was always one big difference, and that was humour. The bitterness of frustration was always sweetened by it.

There were always the small problems to do with communication, especially with the older folk, who had such a beautiful Norfolk accent, and though I was often perplexed at the time, I could always laugh at the incidents, looking back, especially when they involved such characters as Granny Coster. She came into the store one day and walking up to the counter and looking me straight in the eye, said "Cuckoo." "Cuckoo?" I answered. "Cuckoo." said Granny. I looked round at the other customers for help. A housewife spoke up. "Cuckoo." she said. I turned to Maggie, but she shrugged and shook her head. "Cuckoo, Cuckoo," said the customers, all around the shop. "It must be a plot to drive me mad." I whispered to Maggie. Then one young lady went to a shelf, and taking down a tin, handed it to Granny. Granny banged the tin of cocoa down in front of me and pointed to it. "Cuckoo," she said.

"Now I'll have some streaky bacon and some bacon powder," she stated. I thought hard as I got her bacon. It was no good, I was stumped. "Er, what does one use this bacon powder for, Granny?" I asked nervously. "Bacon," she said, with impeccable logic. The young lady came to the rescue once again, and going to the shelves, handed me a small drum which had its name printed on the side. It was baking powder.

It might have been the state of my nerves after this, or the sight of the can of soup that Granny was holding, but when I heard the old lady mumbling something about a "Night soup visor." I took the bait at once, and turned to Maggie. "I suppose," I said, some of my irritation showing in my voice, "that I'm quite mistaken in assuming that a night soup visor is some special type of headgear worn by the inhabitants of this village as they spoon down their bedtime portions of oxtail." Before Maggie could remonstrate with me for being so touchy, Granny interrupted, with a grin and a cackle. "I was only talking about my nephew," she said. "He's got a good job down at the factory where they can this stuff. He's the night soup visor."

Such small misunderstanding only seemed to be irritating at the time, and usually ended in laughter, but I must admit that the locals spent a great deal more time laughing at me than I did at them. But even when some bigger problem arose, it usually ended in humour, not anger. One such problem came about when I tried to save money by cutting corners, and it didn't work.

We had been living in the village for a couple of years when the village policeman set me thinking with a few casual remarks. "You know, you really ought to have a burglar alarm fitted," said P.C. Danby, leaning on the Post Office counter and absent-mindedly helping himself to a jelly baby from the nearby display of sweets. "A few years ago, a little old village store like this, miles away from anywhere, would be as safe as houses, if you know what I mean. But nowadays, when every young tearaway has a car or a motorbike, things are a bit different. You could be broken into by some villain who lives miles away, and he could be back home and in his bed before you even knew that you'd been done." I sighed, and nodded. "I know, and I've thought about it," I said, "but these modern security systems are so expensive, and I haven't convinced myself yet that the risk justifies the outlay." "It would be justified all right if it saved you from being robbed," said Danby.

Maggie, who had been eavesdropping on the conversation, bade farewell to the couple of customers that she had been serving and came over and joined us. "Couldn't you fix up some sort of an alarm yourself?" she asked, with an expression that suggested that such a task should be as simple for me as baking an apple pie was to her. Danby grinned, and raised an eyebrow. "Don't you think," I said, trying to sound hurt, "that after working for six days per week, and most evenings, that I've done enough, without fiddling about with electrical equipment that I don't even understand?" "It's an idea though," said Danby, munching another jelly baby thoughtfully. "A do-it-yourself job might be worth considering. A large bell and a few wires, stuck up outside, where everybody could see them might put off any young amateur who was weighing the place up, and the real professional would hardly be interested in a place like this, would he?" He cast a disparaging glance around the store. "No," he said, swallowing the remains of the jelly baby and popping another one into his mouth. "There isn't enough here to make it worth his while." I was stung by this, and answered him far too quickly, without thinking. "I'll have you know," I said, huffily, "that this shop is absolutely crammed with expensive stock, and there's even more of it in the stockroom behind." "Ah," said Danby with a satisfied smile. "Then you agree with me after all. You do need a burglar alarm." I opened my mouth, but closed it again without speaking. Maggie didn't exactly laugh, but she did give a rather polite little snort. "I'll think about it and let you know later," I said to Danby. "Now, would you care for a jelly baby, before you go?" "No, thanks," said Danby, frowning at the sweets. "I don't care for the look of them."

It was while we were having lunch that Maggie had her bright idea. She had obviously been thinking about Danby's advice, and didn't want the topic to grow cold. "What about Joe the Welk?" she asked. "What about Joe the Welk?" I answered, putting down the newspaper with a show of reluctance, as if I really could have finished the crossword if she hadn't interrupted me. "He's brilliant with anything electrical." said Maggie. "Cars, washing machines, televisions, he can do anything. I'm sure he could fix up some simple alarm system, and he wouldn't charge you the earth." "Hmm. Do you know,

I think you might have something there," I said, as I brought the character in question back to mind. Joseph Welkechenski had suddenly turned up in our remote village some months ago, a mysterious emigrant from some obscure mid-European country. He had quickly obtained work and lodgings on one of the local farms, and though he proved to be a valued employee, it very soon became apparent to all that the foreigner had been something other than a mere farm worker in his homeland. His skill with anything electrical was prodigious, but in spite of his obvious intelligence, and his most painstaking efforts, he found the intricacies of the English language almost impossible to master. This gave the villagers endless amusement, especially when he tried to make small talk on his many visits to the shop, and said such things as, "Today is coldest, yah? The fingers of mine feet is froze."

Joseph took all the leg-pulling and laughter with such great good humour that he soon became popular with one and all, and he attended almost every social function that took place in the village. In spite of his difficulty in communicating with the opposite sex, he also attended each and every one of the barn dances that were such a regular feature of village life. It was at one of these dances, surrounded by his workmates and friends, that Joseph announced that he had become a British citizen, and that he had also changed his name, adopting what he considered to be a more English abbreviation of his own original one. "I am no more Joseph Welkechenski," he announced proudly. "I am now Joe Welk." "Welk?" said his friends, "That's not English, it's not even a proper name." "Oh, yah, is very so." said Joe. "Is sounding most very English to foreign peoples." "Well, all right then, from now on you're a whelk." said his workmate. and the company roared with laughter. From that moment on, Joe was known to everyone in the village as Joe the Welk. He didn't mind in the least. With his usual good humour he accepted that this was the name that his friends had chosen for him, and he was content.

At one of the dances, Joe saw, and fell for, one of the local girls, a farmer's daughter, and it was then that his failure to grasp the basics of the English language really began to affect his life. After following the girl around for half the evening, and eventually plucking up enough courage to speak to her, he found that she couldn't make any sense at all of the broken English that he had learnt to use in order to communicate with his friends. Her speech also baffled him. Words of more than one or two syllables was incomprehensible to Joe, and his staccato monosyllables were equally incomprehensible to the girl. Joe was disconsolate, and confided in his workmates the next day. Laboriously he conveyed his feelings for the girl to his friends, and begged their assistance in communicating his emotions to the young lady herself. His friends obliged willingly, though not without a certain amount of smirking and winking at each other. During their lunchbreaks they taught Joe to repeat, parrot fashion, several phrases that they considered suitable to be uttered by a man of his mental stature, such as, "I love every hair of your head." and "The beauty of your body fascinates me." They all agreed that these were not the sort of remarks that they themselves would ever use, but the general opinion was that Joe was not the sort of man who would wish to approach a girl with, "Do you come here often?"

Joe repeated the words over and over to himself as he went about his work around the farm, striving to pronounce the words without a trace of accent, but never fully understanding the meaning of what he was saying. He startled one burly visiting lorry driver by walking up behind him and talking softly about his beautiful body, and one itinerant salesman packed up his samples and fled, after Joe's voice had repeatedlv assured him that the hairs on his head were being loved.

Joe persevered, the image of the farmer's daughter in her dance dress bright in his mind's eye. On the evening of the next dance, Joe turned up early and went straight to the bar, intending to fortify himself for the coming ordeal with a small drink. He was not a drinking man normally, and he placed his trust in his more experienced friends. On this occasion however, his trust in his workmates was misplaced. Not only did Joe fail to understand the English language, he also failed to understand the Englishman's sense of humour. His friends plied him with drink after drink, as he repeated the well-worn phrases again and again, until Joe no longer knew what he was doing, or more important, what he was saying.

He missed all the dancing, and still sitting at the bar, only remembered his important mission at the very last minute, when the last waltz was being played, and the single men were vying with each other for the privilege of escorting the eligible girls homeward. Joe left the bar and swayed across the floor towards the sturdily built young woman who was the girl of his dreams. He stood and waited politely for her to finish a conversation that she was having with a girl friend, and the young lady noted his presence. She stopped talking, and gave the bleary eyed male a withering look. She vaguely recollected Joe's incoherent advances from a previous meeting, and being nettled by the fact that no young man had offered to escort her home, was in no mood to be troubled by this man's tiresome talk again.

"What are you staring at?" the girl demanded. Joe pulled himself together, and reaching far back into his rapidly failing memory, blurted out the well rehearsed words. "I am fascinated by the shape of your head." he said, "And I love all those hairs on your body."

Joe stood, smiling expectantly, awaiting what he had been assured would be a romantic response to his words. If he was very lucky, she might fling her arms around him, overcome by the poetry of his words, but surely, the very least that he could expect would be that she would give him a warm smile. What she did in fact was to give him a powerful right hook that draped him across the dancefloor like a wet dishcloth, and loosened his front teeth. Joe's smile was never quite the same after that.

Joe's love for the girl weathered this minor setback, and after the young lady had been present in the Post Office at the same time as Joe on a couple of occasions, she came to realise, from his painful attempts to explain his requirements, and all the leg-pulling from the other customers, that it was merely his difficulty with the language that had caused the misunderstanding. She was greatly touched by the manner in which the modest foreigner accepted all the jokes at his expense, and in a fit of remorse at her hasty attack on him, she offered to try to teach him better English. Joe naturally leapt at the chance; they met regularly, and romance blossomed after all. Joe was happy. He had his girl, and his English was improving, if ever so slowly. But he did still have a lot of trouble with those front teeth.

After Maggie's suggestion, I went to see Joe and put the problem of the burglar alarm to him. He was only too eager to help, and assured me that he could carry out such a simple task quickly. He was as good as his word, and only three days after Maggie had brought up his name, we had our alarm system fully installed. Joe complained, all the time that he was working, about his aching front teeth, and though Maggie had rummaged through her collection of pills that all ex-nurses seem to have, and willingly given him something to ease the pain, she had told him repeatedly that he must visit a dentist, and get professional advice. Joe didn't seem to like that idea at all.

The alarm system was an extremely simple one, once it had been explained to us. Outside, at the front of the shop, high up on the wall, there was an enormous bell. Inside, in both the shop and the house, there was a system of switches, one on each door and window. Once the system had been switched on, anyone opening a door or window would automatically set the bell ringing. We did have a little trouble, right at the start when Joe himself accidentally triggered the alarm while showing me how to operate it. The noise from the bell was almost unbearable, and the vibrations from it set the pointer on the shop scales quivering, and brought down flakes of plaster from the ceiling. By the time that Joe had managed to stop the awful clanging, almost every villager had gathered outside the closed shop, some with shotguns, some with dogs, and worst of all, some with hammers and wire cutters, intent on stopping the terrible noise, whatever the cause or consequence.

P.C. Danby was the last person to answer the insistent call of the alarm. He had heard the dreadful bell from his hiding place in the woods, almost two miles away, where he had been hoping to apprehend a poacher. He appeared to be quite unreasonably disappointed at having been called away to a false alarm, and wouldn't eat even one jelly baby when I offered them. One would almost have thought that he would have preferred us to have been actually robbed, though he did have a quiet word with one irate villager who was seen taking aim at the bell with his twelve bore shotgun.

After a good deal of explaining and apologising, we managed to get the crowd to disperse, and then I paid Joe the Welk for his work, and sent him on his way. All was peaceful again, and Maggie and I prepared to turn in for the night. Maggie went upstairs ahead of me, and I was about to follow her when I remembered that I had left some invoices in the stockroom, and that I simply had to check them before going to bed. I opened the stockroom door, and at once that terrible sound told me what I had done. I had set the thing off again.

Fewer people turned out this time, and I wasn't quite sure whether I should be pleased or not by this. After all, I could have been involved in a life or death struggle with a gang of criminals, for all the stay-aways knew. I did receive a few phone calls from friends and neighbours who seemed to have suddenly lost their sense of humour, and Danby turned up again eventually, breathless, and looking oddly tired, I thought. I managed to stop the clanging of the bell, and explained what had happened. Danby didn't speak very much at all on this visit, and he refused the offered jelly babies with what could have easily have been mistaken for ill-temper by someone who didn't know him as well as I did.

We had no trouble with the alarm the next day, at least not after I had switched it off after the first brief clanging when I opened up the shop. We did have a few muttered comments from one farmer about the effect of sudden noises on his hens, and their egg-laying routine, but as I bought most of his eggs from him anyway, I paid him an outstanding account, and he seemed to be satisfied.

After work I set off in the car to collect a few cases of bankrupt stock that I had managed to pick up cheaply, switching on the alarm system before I went, and telling Maggie that I wouldn't be long. I left, feeling confident that Maggie would feel a lot safer alone in the place, now that the alarm system had been installed, and so thoroughly tested. Maggie didn't. She sat petrified on a stool in the kitchen, afraid to move an inch lest she should set off that awful noise again.

I was away for longer than I had intended, and evening wore into night. Darkness fell, and Maggie, sitting alone in the kitchen suddenly heard the sound of faint footsteps outside the kitchen door. "Hello, is that you?" she called, expecting me to answer. All that came back was a faint moaning sound, an almost animal-like noise. There was a scrabbling at the door, and the sound of feet again. Maggie might have been afraid of upsetting the neighbours with the noise of the bell, but was most certainly not afraid of tackling any intruder who dared to enter her house and home. She took up her rolling pin, and stood by the door, quietly listening. The door handle turned, and she remembered that she hadn't locked it after I had left. The door inched open slightly, and then suddenly, that infernal bell began its metallic clanging. The door swung wide, and on the doorstep, half in and half out of the light, stood a figure. It was the figure of a strange man, and most of his face was covered by some sort of mask. He blinked at the light for a second, and Maggie didn't hesitate. With all the force of her five foot nothing, seven and a half stone physique, she crashed her rolling pin down on the intruder's head. The figure gave out another strangled animal noise, and then lost his powers of speech for a while, as overcome by a desire to lie down, he folded his legs under him and laid his weary head down on the threshold.

Dogs were barking again, and torches flashing through the darkness. A near-riotous gang of neighbours appeared, their anger understandable at having been disturbed again, and so late at night. Their anger turned from their village sub-postmaster to the intruder, once they saw him lying there, with Maggie standing over him, rolling pin at the ready. Rough hands grasped the criminal, and hauled him to his feet. They ripped off the scarf that had been hiding the lower part of his face, and then looked at each other in surprise. The well known features of Joe the Welk were revealed, and he stood swaying on his feet, and blinking round at his captors in terror. "Lady," he said in pleading tones to Maggie, "tis me. I come to show you no teeth, look." he gave a toothless and bloody grin, and Maggie recoiled, but still gripped the rolling pin tightly.

"I have taking your advice," explained Joe. "I am coming to be showing, not to be stealing." Someone in the crowd began to chuckle, and then another, and in a few seconds the whole crowd were slapping their thighs and roaring with laughter, while Joe the Welk looked round in bewilderment, and rubbed his aching head. Then Danby arrived again, strangely weary, and quelling the mirth with a grim glance, began asking questions, rather half heartedly.

By the time I arrived home the incident was over. Joe had shown no ill-feelings towards Maggie, but like the gentleman that he was had kept on apologising over and over for the trouble that he had caused. He had stopped the bell ringing, and after Maggie had given him a couple of tablets for his aching gums, and his aching head, he had left. The villagers had also gone back to their homes, and only Danby was left on the premises. He seemed surprisingly good natured about the whole affair, in spite of his obvious fatigue, for he did keep yawning and rubbing his eyes. He even insisted on looking round the whole premises before he left, to see if there were any weaknesses in our security arrangements. As he cast an eye around the shop, I again offered the jelly babies to him. "No thanks," he said, "but I am partial to a bit of chewing gum every now and then. It seems to soothe the nerves." I gave him what

I hoped was an understanding smile, and handed him two packets.

"I'll just have a quick look round upstairs now." said Danby. "I'll make sure that no-one can gain entry by one of the upper windows." "Feel free," I said. "I'll go and unload that carful of stuff that I brought back." "And I'll have a cup of tea ready when you've both finished," said Maggie, and headed for the kitchen.

We had no trouble at all with the alarm for a long time after that. The days went by, and there was never a false alert. Then one day I accidentally triggered the switch on the shop door. I winced, and clapped my hands over my ears in anticipation, but nothing happened. The bell didn't ring. I checked the wiring, not too sure what it was that I was looking for, but I could find no obvious fault. I was concerned. It could be that some criminal had sabotaged the system, with the intention of breaking in during the night. On the other hand, it could be just a simple fault. I needed help, and so I sent a hasty message to Joe the Welk. The same evening, he turned up. He took a quick look at the switch, and shook his head, then went upstairs. He opened a bedroom window, and leaning out, examined the bell on the wall. "Ah, yes, is here," he called. "Sis is the stopping thing." I leaned out and looked. The hammer of the bell was actually moving, but it was making no sound because it was being prevented from striking the bell by some obstruction. "Yah, very so," said Joe. "I think that some peoples has been leaning out of from window and putting sis in bell." He reached out and pulled the obstruction away from the hammer. The bell began its familiar clanging once more, this time painfully at such close quarters. "I tink you must been having some naughty little boy in here," said Joe, yelling over the din of the bell as he fingered the substance that he had removed. "Look, sis stuff is chewing gum."

42

CHAPTER THREE

THANKSGIVING.

In our previous life in the city, Maggie and I had noticed the changing seasons of each year, but without any particular enthusiasm. We had welcomed spring, of course, and grumbled at winter, but our lives had continued in very much the same way, whatever the season. In our new life in the remoteness of the village we found that each season brought a change that was significant, and also pleasurable. We learnt to enjoy the hardest winter days, and even the rain that came in summer too. Harvest time, which had slipped by unnoticed in the city, became a particularly important part of the year, and almost as great a celebration as Christmas.

A change came over the countryside as harvest got under way, and a change came over the villagers too. There was a strange excitement and urgency about. Old men stood and looked at the sky, and with one wet finger tried to forecast the weather for the next few days. Farmers who had previously taken advantage of every opportunity to gossip and while away a pleasant half hour now hauled out their watches and, cutting conversation dead, hurried away to the fields, while their wives popped in and out of the village stores with polite but abrupt requests for sticking plasters and calomine lotion.

The fields themselves, that had stood for so long, waving their mantles of slowly maturing beauty, and hiding a teeming population of animal life, now altered overnight. Each separate field became a golden sunlit scene, where brown skinned men played their parts from dawn till dusk, while old men with small dogs stood patiently in the wings, waiting to snap up any rabbits and rats that fled the stage.

The weather usually held, but the farmers usually grumbled, as farmers will, and whatever the weather brought, the harvest was always eventually brought in. Once it was all over, and the women were back in their kitchens and the children back to their studies, almost every member of the village community made their way to the village church, for the Harvest Festival service, the service of Thanksgiving. During our second year of village life, Maggie and I went along too.

To us two city-born people it was such a typically English scene, an ageless scene: the little flint church, standing in the golden stubble of the cornfields, its old clock showing different times on each of its four faces; the row of bicycles, leant carelessly against the churchyard wall; the black cat drowsing on a sun-warmed gravestone. It was a scene of perfect, unbroken peace. We mentioned this to each other as we strolled up the path, but we were wrong, as we so often were. The scene might have been peaceful on the surface, but beneath, there were unsuspected currents.

Long before the service was due to start, the villagers began to arrive, in twos and threes and family groups.

They carried flowers with them, and garden produce, vegetables and fruit, and even cheeses, bottles of home made wine, and small, hand worked gifts. Against the altar rails there were trestle tables, arranged in a row and covered with spotless white linen. The offerings were laid there carefully, even reverently, by the villagers, and then they were arranged expertly by two matrons of the community who always volunteered their services on such occasions. Corn dollies glowed dully on the cloth, and a pair of rabbits lay limply against a backdrop of ripe red apples and russet pears. The feet shuffled past in a continuous stream and soon the church was so full that it began to lose its echoes, and the boards on the trestles groaned beneath their load.

Granny Coster, a dear old lady but noted for her eccentricity, shuffled past, nodding and cackling to herself as she eyed the offerings. Before she turned away, she fumbled in the pockets of her dusty black coat, and placed a sticky and rather grimy ball of paper on the edge of the table. She moved along, and poked at the two rabbits with the umbrella that she usually carried, whatever the weather. One of the helpers gave the other one a meaningful glance, and picking up the paper, unwrapped it, cautiously. "It's humbugs," she whispered to her friend. "It's a bag of humbugs." She hastened round to where Granny was squeezing an over-ripe pear. "You've forgotten your sweets," she said, holding out the bag with the tips of her fingers. "Oh no I ain't," said Granny, with a cackle that turned quite a few heads. "Them's me thanksgiving offering." "Oh," said the helper, then held out the sweets once again. "It's a nice thought, but I'm sure that they'll be of more use to you than to us. They'll do you good, especially if you've got a cough." "That they won't," snapped Granny. "Ain't you ever watched the telly?" The helper looked puzzled. She wasn't to know that Granny had only recently acquired a television set, for the first time in her life, and though she regarded the programmes as "a load of old squit", she watched the adverts avidly, believing every word of them. "It's them stripes," she whispered to the helper, "I'll never eat 'em agin, 'cos of them. They've got deodorant in 'em." She shuffled away, leaving the helper holding the bag.

Weasel Peters, a small brown man with quick movements and a nervous expression, came into the church breathlessly, an object of some considerable size bulging beneath his brown tweed jacket. He didn't join the stream of people who were entering by the front door, but came in quickly by the side entrance, looking back over his shoulder as he came. Then he shuffled his way into the stream of worshippers, in between a group of schoolchildren and a burly farmer and his family of bronzed young giants. As he passed the tables, Weasel hastily produced a cock pheasant that he had been hiding beneath his coat, and placing it down, went and stood panting in the gloomiest part of the church. A few of the regular churchgoers raised their eyebrows at each other as they saw him, and noted the pheasant. Weasel wasn't often seen at services, apart from the odd wedding or funeral. His part-time occupation of poacher usually kept him busy at those times when good Christian people were about their devotions.

The organ started, very quietly. The village schoolmistress, who was playing, hadn't been called upon to perform that task for some months, and she was anxious to renew her acquaintance with the instrument before the service itself began. She ran through a few of the best known hymns, and the children of the choir, grateful for anything that relieved the awful monotony of waiting, began to join in, one by one. A few of them rose to their feet, and then a few parents followed their example. More adults joined them, and soon the whole of the congregation was standing and singing enthusiastically. The organist smiled, and played slightly louder. The old men leant on their sticks and mouthed the words, their memories bringing slight smiles to their faces as they did so. The womenfolk, their tanned faces glowing against crisply ironed blouses, sang the words from memory, while their husbands, hot and uncomfortable in collars and ties and strange suits, held hymn books in work-thickened fingers, and took breaths that strained the buttons on their shirts as they sang. The children, with the sunlight streaming on their shining hair and shining cheeks, sang like angels, innocent of their effect, while grandparents, with equally shining eyes, heaved deep sighs, and blinked mistily as they listened. Maggie and I joined in, and smiled happily to each other as we looked around. It was a scene of such perfect harmony, such peace.

The vicar entered, bringing into the church what must have been the palest face in the whole village. The organist noticed his presence, and the music faded away. The voices trailed off one by one. The two helpers left the row of tables and took their places in the pews. Weasel Peters stopped panting at last, and sat down, and the service began.

The vicar was in the pulpit when P.C. Danby, the village policeman and expert poacher catcher, came into the church by the side door. He stood for a moment, just inside the doorway, his brow damp, his uniform clinging uncomfortably to him. He ran a large finger around the inside of his collar and looked around the church, as his eyes began to adjust to the relative gloom. He saw the produce piled high on the tables, the splashes of bright colour as the sunlight streamed through the stained glass window and fell like a spotlight on the white cloth. He saw the brilliant plumage of the cock pheasant, and he nodded to himself. "That must be the one," he

thought. The very same pheasant that he had been looking for for the past hour or so, ever since he had made
the unpardonable mistake of allowing himself to doze
off in the warm sun while watching and waiting for the
poacher to come and collect the bird from the snare that
held it. He had woken with a guilty start when the snapping of twigs had penetrated to his sleeping brain, and
had just been in time to see a pair of small brown hands
freeing the pheasant from the noose of the snare. How
the pheasant had managed to get itself caught in what
was after all a rabbit snare, was something of a puzzle
to Danby, but rabbit or pheasant, the snare was an illegal
one, and those hands were the hands of a poacher.

He had leapt to his feet, and the hands had disappeared, taking the pheasant with them, into the leaves
of a bush. Danby had given chase. He had run himself
into a state of near exhaustion, charging around the
copse, vainly trying to cover the several paths that led
back to the road, and pausing every now and again to
listen, then hurrying off in the direction of every rustle
or slight creak. It was during one of these pauses that
he had heard the sound of singing coming across the
stubble from the direction of the church. It had struck
the policeman that the poacher might well have avoided
passing him on the way back to the road by crossing the
field and going into the church by the side door. There
would be quite a large crowd in the church, and that
might be a good place for a man to lose himself.

The sight of the pheasant on the table now told Danby
that he had been right. No wonder that none of the
foraging dogs that were hunting over the stubble fields
had come running with a pheasant dangling from its
jaws. The poacher hadn't discarded the bird at all. He
must have brought it into church with him. Well, that
bird had to be illegal, whoever had placed it there. The
shooting season hadn't started yet, and surely there

would be plenty of people in the congregation who would remember who it was who had placed such an unusual offering on the boards.

He took his gaze from the bird and looked round at the worshippers. His roving eye stopped when it came to Weasel Peters. Ah! A poacher like Weasel, in church, and at this hour? It was just what he might have expected. Those had been Weasel's hands, small and brown, and Danby knew now that whatever happened, he simply had to get his man. If Weasel was allowed to get away with this, the story would be told and retold in every village pub, until it was exaggerated beyond all recognition. He would be made to look a fool, and once that happened, and his authority gone, he would have every amateur poacher for miles around trying his hand on his patch.

The policeman moved quietly forward, trying not to divert attention away from the vicar, who was still speaking so earnestly from the pulpit. He eased himself into the seat at the side of the poacher and placed his hat under the pew. Weasel didn't even turn his head as the bulky policeman slid in beside him, but he did stiffen slightly and stared intently at the man in the pulpit, as though the words that the clergyman was uttering were full of special meaning for him.

"And so the cycle continues," said the vicar, "this miracle that we can all witness with our own eyes, year after year. Each living thing comes to maturity; its cycle is complete. The object has been achieved. Then comes the final stage. The harvest, in the case of the crops in the fields, and death, in the case of animals, and we humans. But that is not the end. It cannot be the end, if there is to be any meaning at all to our lives. Just as with the crops of the fields the next spring will bring a new life, so with us humans, there is another awakening." He paused, and as he did so, a small scream came

49

from one of the children in the front pew. "It's true." shrilled a tiny voice. "It's coming back to life, look at it." A tiny finger pointed, and the other children looked. On the bright white linen of the table, lit by the dust flecked spotlight of the sun, there was movement. The brightly feathered pheasant was no longer lying limply at the foot of a pile of fruit. It was struggling unsteadily to its feet. Its neck had not been broken by the cruel noose. It had not been dead at all. It had merely been unconscious.

Weasel drew an audible breath, and in spite of himself turned and peered at Danby with his small brown eyes. Questions concerning the law were flashing through his mind, but he couldn't very well expect the policeman to provide him with the answers, What difference would the bird's recovery make to the charge of poaching that was surely hanging over him at the moment? Could he be charged at all, he wondered, if he snatched up the apparently unharmed bird and raced back to the copse with it? How would it sound to the magistrates if he swore that he had found the bird injured, in some unknown poacher's snare, and being a deeply religious man, had brought it into the church in order to have it blessed, and had then been rewarded by this minor miracle?

P.C. Danby frowned and rubbed his chin. Thoughts were passing through his mind too. The pheasant's recovery didn't alter a thing, he told himself. A poached pheasant was a poached pheasant, whether alive or dead, but whatever happened, he must now get his hands on that bird. To allow it to escape now would mean that he had no proof at all to place before the magistrates, and if the poacher got away, that would only make his story all the better for telling later.

The bird shook itself, and flapped its wings tentatively. The row of children in the front pews all squealed in chorus. The piles of fruit on the tables shook with the movement of the bird, and then began to move, one pile setting the next in motion. The carefully placed pyramids collapsed, and the fruit rolled from the tables and over the floor, in a bouncing, colourful cascade. The children chortled gleefully, and leaving their seats went down on their hands and knees, scrabbling in their race to collect the fallen fruit. The adults at the back of the church strained on tiptoe to see what was going on, and the vicar stood, dumb-struck and open-mouthed, his words of wisdom forgotten as he watched the scuffling heap of children on the floor.

"Oh Gaw," said Old Charlie loudly. "That's fair ruined that lot, that has. We allus gets the fruit, for the pensioners' club, the day after the service, but they'll be all bruised and soggy by termorrer, after all that." "Them blarsted kids will be all bruised and soggy if they don't stop hurlin the stuff about," said his companion Ben testily. He struck out smartly with his stick at the rear portions of a boy who was grovelling underneath the pew in front. The boy squirmed away from his attacker, and emerged from underneath the pew on all fours. In his haste to extricate himself before the stick was applied for a second time, he reached out and grabbed one of the legs of the trestle in front of him. As he pulled himself forward, the trestle moved, and the planks that it supported fell. Vegetables, fruit and flowers now crashed to the floor in one great avalanche. There was the sound of breaking glass, and the dusty air of the church was filled with the heavy fumes of home-made rhubarb wine. The children regarded this as being all part of the fun, and they gathered up the sticky fruit gleefully and replaced it on the remaining tables. As they went down on their hands and knees once more, the replaced fruit rolled to the edge and dropped off again. The congregation watched in awe.

This cycle of events threatened to become a never-ending source of entertainment unless something was done to put an end to it. The vicar did nothing, but stared in dismay. One boisterous lad deposited an armful of fruit with more enthusiasm than dexterity, and the apples rolled along the table and came into contact with a tall vase of flowers. There were several such vases, and the first one fell sideways onto the next, sending all the others crashing one by one.

The pheasant, now fully alert, and considerably alarmed at finding itself in such an unusual environment, heard the crashes, and with a rattle of alarm in its throat, hurled itself into the air. With wildly flailing wings it powered its heavy body towards an open window. Danby, now seeing the distinct possibility of his only evidence disappearing before his eyes, leapt to his feet and made a frantic grab at the bird as it passed overhead. His regulation boots came down heavily on a couple of Cox's Orange Pippins that had rolled down the aisle, and as they turned to pulp beneath him, his feet skidded. He staggered back, out of control, and sat down clumsily, right in the lap of an amply proportioned widow in the pew behind. The widow instinctively threw her arms about the policeman to prevent the two of them falling to the floor, then she froze in that position, with her dark eyes staring deep into Danbys.

Against everyone's expectations, the pheasant reached the window, and paused there on the sill, recovering from its exertions. Danby gave the widow a sickly smile, and prised himself loose from her embrace. He tiptoed to the window, and gathering himself for the effort, made one last desperate leap up the wall. Perhaps if he had been fresh, he might have made it, but he had already expended more than one days fair share of energy, and the soles of his boots were still thick with crushed apple. The window was just a little too high for

him, and he slid down the wall, and crouched there, panting, until the muscular arms of the widow reached out to him once more, and hauled him to his feet.

The vicar still watched as though in some sort of

trance. His service was now in ruins. The two volunteer helpers hurried back to the tables, and quietening the children as best they could, began to stack the produce once more, as neatly as haste would allow. "Are you quite sure that these two aren't going to get up and start running about?" asked one helper of her colleague, as she pointed warily at the two limp rabbits. "Oh, no. They're stone dead all right," said her friend. "You can put that cucumber down." The first helper stopped brandishing the cucumber like a weapon, and placed it back on the table. Then, after giving the two rabbits another suspicious look, she moved it further away from them.

The schoolteacher sat at the organ, her hands paused over the keys, awaiting some sign from the vicar that she should start to play again. The vicar gave no sign. He still stood like a statue.

The pheasant sat on the window sill, and Danby wasn't quite beaten yet. "Quick, you lot," he said to the crowd of children. "That pheasant mustn't be allowed to escape, whatever happens. Go outside and give it a scare so that it flies back into the church." The children looked at him gravely. "Is it under arrest then?" asked one boy, absent-mindedly chewing an apple that he had just retrieved from under the pew. "Is it a jailbird?" asked his small friend. "Don't be impertinent," said Danby. "It's evidence, and it's very important. Now off you go, and if you manage to get it back inside, I might manage to forget about all those apples that you all keep on eating." The children trooped out of the church by the side door. Some of the parents, seeing their offspring leaving, and still not knowing the reason why, pushed their way after them. Other adults at the far back, not understanding at all what was going on, followed them outside, determined not to miss anything. The vicar stood and watched them go, his pale face now even paler then ever. There were now more of his congregation outside the church than in.

An apple flew through the air. It missed the sitting bird and shot through the window, and striking the edge of the pulpit, showered bits of juicy pulp onto the vicar's vestments. The vicar twitched slightly, but remained in his stupor. A second apple flew, and falling short of the first, fell amongst the pensioners. "Hey," gasped Old Charlie, peering round short-sightedly. "This ain't on. I ain't a-standing about here to be an Aunt Sally for anybody." He made as if to leave the pew, but a voice of authority stopped him in his tracks. "Stand your ground, man," barked the ex-sergeant behind him. "Never let a feeling of panic prevent you from performing your duty." He drew himself erect, and gripping his hymn book, threw out his chest. "After all," he said, his old eyes gleaming with recollection, "If an apple's got your number on it...." He didn't finish the sentence, as a small red pippin took him cleanly in the teeth, unseating his dentures. He dropped swiftly to his knees, and lowered his head, as if praying hard. "Of coursh, in the old daysh," his voice came gummily, "we did have shteel helmetsh."

Another apple flew, and this time struck the frame of the window. The sitting pheasant gave out a raucous squawk, and launched itself into the air once more. It began losing height almost immediately, in spite of its frantically beating wings, but it did just manage to clear the stubble field and glide clumsily into the shade of the copse that was its home.

Inside the church, Danby watched the bird's departure with set teeth and a muttered phrase that was meant for no other ears but his own. Weasel caught the policeman's expression, and a wide grin spread over his small face. The schoolteacher, seeing that chaos was likely to reign for some time unless action was taken,

55

looked at the vicar, and then taking matters into her own hands, struck up the organ once again. The air was filled with the strains of a familiar hymn, and the crowd outside, after watching the pheasant disappearing into the distance, began to filter back into the church, and take up their hymn books.

"Ah, yes," said the vicar, pulling himself together with an effort. He had completely lost the thread of his sermon, but he too recognised the tune that the organ was playing. "All is safely gathered in," he said. "That's right." Danby prised his arm free from the widow's grasping fingers once more, and stood and glowered at Weasel. The widow rose and stood at the policeman's side, and she too gave the poacher a look that would have struck fear into the hearts of most men. "Not all, vicar," growled Danby. "Not all. There's still one that ain't gathered in yet."

"Er, thanksgiving," said the vicar, pretending that he hadn't heard the remark. He forced a smile as he looked around at the congregation. They had begun to settle in their pews again, and some of them had begun to sing, if somewhat half-heartedly. "That is, after all, why we are all gathered here today, to give thanksgiving. Now, let us all sing together, and can we try to forget this little disturbance, and concentrate on the meaning of the words. Let us all sing as though we really mean it."

The voices rose together, and the sound spilled out of the little church and over the golden fields. The sun still shone. The cat still drowsed on the gravestone. It was still the same ageless, peaceful scene. In all the voices that gave thanks, one could be heard above all the rest. Weasel Peters at least, sang out his thanksgiving as though he really meant it. The widow's voice was pretty loud, too.

CHAPTER FOUR.

A DEAL OF BUSINESS.

"You know, if we were to offer a delivery service to some of the more remote farms and smallholdings," said Maggie, as she looked around at the almost empty shop on a particularly quiet Tuesday morning, "we might draw in quite a lot of extra business." Tuesdays were always rather quiet, and I didn't mind at all. I knew that the shop would be almost too busy for us to cope for the rest of the week. "Oh, I don't think that idea would work," I said. "It's a very expensive business nowadays, running a delivery service. With cut prices and competition from the supermarkets, the profit margin on general groceries just isn't high enough to stand the cost, that's why deliveries died out." "Well, how about a free delivery for orders over a certain size, and a delivery charge for anything smaller?" she said. "Hmm," I said, wondering to myself just what was going on in her mind. "What gave you this idea, all of a sudden?" "Well, it would be a good thing for us if it worked," she said.

"And?" I asked. "And we do happen to know of an excellent driver, who is absolutely trustworthy, and who is looking for ways of earning a little extra money, and who is available towards the end of each week, which is just when we would need him." "Oh, now I see," I said. "Young Sandy. You're fond of the lad and his girl friend, and you want us to help him to save up to get married." "He is such a nice young man, and he does work so hard," said Maggie. "He deserves to get on, but apart from that, any increase in trade would be welcome, wouldn't it?" "You know, there's a very well known old saying, about business and sentiment," I said. "But I promise to think the thing over, and if there's any chance at all that it can be profitable, then we'll give it a try. I'll chew it over as I'm driving to the wholesalers this afternoon."

On my way to the city I pulled up at a filling station, and got out while the attendant was filling the tank with petrol. With Maggie's delivery idea vaguely in my mind I took a casual look at a battered old van that was standing listlessly on the forecourt, with a *For Sale* sign optimistically displayed on its windscreen. If the scheme was to go ahead, I would be needing some sort of van, but it had to be both cheap and reliable. This van should be cheap enough, judging by its age and condition, but was it in sound mechanical condition? I wished that I knew more about the workings of mechanical things, and wondered if I could bluff the attendant into telling me a little of the van's history.

The salesman crept up behind me as I pondered, like a cat stalking its prey, and then he pounced. "Good afternoon, General," he said, and I jumped. "A little beauty, isn't she?" he said, and patted the rusted wing of the van affectionately. The van rocked sideways with surprising violence, and something out of sight rattled loudly. The salesman stopped patting, and cleared his throat. "Have a look inside, Colonel," he said. "No obligation, of course." He flashed a set of professional teeth, and swung the van door open with a flourish. The door didn't stop where it should have, but swung right round and clanged against the side of the body. A screw fell at his feet, then the door handle also fell to the ground. "That's nothing at all to worry about," he said, smiling again. "A mere detail, easily fixed, you know." He began to fiddle with the screw and the handle. I got into the driving seat, and the van heeled over at an alarming angle. As the van slumped, the salesman had to crouch lower and lower as he tried to replace the handle. Eventually, he gave up the struggle, and coming round to the other side of the van, crept into the passenger seat, holding the small of his back as he did so. The door handle was still in his hand.

As soon as the salesman got in, the van stopped leaning over, and righted itself, but it did continue to rock gently from side to side for quite a while. I turned the key that was already in its place in the dashboard. The engine grumbled lazily at being disturbed, but it didn't start. "Try a bit of the old choke, Major," said the salesman, and reaching over, he pulled out the knob on the dash. The knob came away in his hand, trailing wire behind it. "A mere detail," he smiled again. "Soon fixed, you know." I tried the wind screen wipers, for want of something better to do. They moved, if somewhat sluggishly, but at the end of each sweep, the horn sounded briefly. "A slight short there, Captain," said the salesman. "Another detail," I suggested. "Easily fixed." "Yes, you're right," he beamed. "I can see that you know a thing or two about vans. Still, it's a shame in a way, you know. That could be very useful in town driving, for frightening pedestrians."·

I mused. I had noticed with interest my rapid demotion from the rank of General, and could hardly wait to see how the salesman would address me next. I decided that if he addressed me as Corp, or Sarge, then I would be, in his view, completely under his command, as he doubtlessly considered himself to be officer material. "We can put all these little things right in a half a day, that is, if you are interested in the van, er, mister," he said. I felt relieved. I'd been demobbed, and was at least free to make my own decisions. I got out and walked slowly around the rocking van. I peered underneath every now and again, and shook my head. I didn't know what it was that I was looking for, but thought that it looked good. I kicked the tyres, as I'd seen the experts do, I winced as my corns stabbed pain, and wondered why the devil they did it.

I looked at the waiting salesman, and shook my head sadly, as though I had spotted many faults. "I'm not really interested." I said. "It's not worth a lot, is it?" "We're not asking a lot." said the salesman. I looked at the van doubtfully. "Just how cheap would it be, after all the little details had been put right?" I asked. "A hundred and fifty, er, sir." he said. The words had been waiting ready on the tip of his tongue. I tried to look as if I'd lost all interest. I knew that I should haggle, that it was expected of me, but I didn't know where to begin. "No, I'm sorry." I said. "It's not worth a penny more than a hundred to me." "Done." the salesman snapped, and grasped my hand fiercely to seal the deal before I could change my mind. He dropped the door handle on my corns as he did so. "She'll be waiting, all ready for the road, tomorrow morning, er, mate."

The sign that Maggie had written, and displayed in the shop, advertising the new delivery service, seemed to have worked. We had received several orders, and most of them were pretty big ones. I began to see that this scheme of hers might after all build up into something that was quite worthwhile. Young Sandy, having

60

been offered the part time job by Maggie had accepted eagerly, and had turned up on time, and was raring to go. The van was parked outside the shop, and Sandy was loading up with cartons of groceries, when a farmer customer came in and nodded towards the rusty vehicle. "You only just beat me to it," he said. "I've been looking out for one of them for weeks. There aren't many of them about nowadays, you know. I wish I'd been quicker off the mark." I gave Maggie a triumphant look. She had turned white when I had told her how much I had paid for the van, and had said several times that in her opinion it wasn't worth any more than a tenner. "Oh, I know just how you must feel," I said to the farmer, speaking extra loudly, so that Maggie couldn't fail to hear. "I'm like you, I suppose, I know a bargain when I see one."

As it stood at the kerb, with its engine ticking over noisily, the van shook and rattled so much that it actually changed the shape of its profile by the minute. The wings and bonnet seemed to be connected to the rest of the van by some kind of loose hinges, so that they could move independently of each other and the body. The exhaust wagged like the tail of an over-affectionate dog. Sandy finished loading, and climbed aboard enthusiastically. He didn't comment when the van tilted over, or when the boxes in the back then slid to one side, increasing the list. He started the engine. The van sank back on its rusty haunches and gathered itself. Then it sprang forward up the road, with its battered members flapping, like some gigantic rust-red hen. It still listed heavily towards the crown of the road as it went, bright blue smoke trailing in its wake. I nodded in approval as I watched it go, but for some strange reason, Maggie stood and shook her head.

Sandy came to the level crossing where the railway crossed the village street. The gates were closed. The van muttered and fumed, and then trembled with what could have been rage as it waited. The blue smoke that had trailed out behind now filtered into the van as it was standing, and Sandy was seized with a terrible coughing fit. He wound the window down, and stuck his head out, his eyes streaming. When the gates were eventually opened, and the van went forward, it left such a cloud of smoke hanging over the lines that the old gateman, sniffing appreciatively, stood for a moment, smiling to himself. "Bor, it fair takes you back to the old days," he said. "When all them old steam trains used to come through here, they all smelled just like that."

Once over the crossing, Sandy, who had boasted to Maggie and I that he knew the whole area like the back of his hand, turned off the main road and into the maze of narrow lanes that ran like spiders webs over the landscape. He intended to make a good impression on his first trip, and deliver all the orders in as short a time as possible. His plan didn't go well, as ten minutes later he was still searching for the first address, and the green lane that he was driving along was getting narrower by the second. He passed a large, obviously home-made sign, saying "PRIVATE PROPERTY", but as he didn't have enough room to turn the van, and it was too far to reverse back along his tracks, he had no option but to go slowly ahead.

The lane came to a dead end at a thatched cottage, where a man, a tall and sinewy rustic, was working on the garden, digging methodically, and with a ferocity that was alarming to behold. Sandy came to a stop, and stuck his head out of the window, intending to apologise for the intrusion, and to explain that he was lost, and ask for directions. He didn't get the chance. The gardener made sure of that. "Can't you read?" he yelled. "Hop it, and quick." Sandy weighed up the build of the man, and his expression, and all thoughts of a rude response went. He executed a rapid three-point turn, and sped back along the lane. The bad-tempered gardener watched him as he went, weighing the spade thoughtfully in his strong hands as he did so.

Sandy went back to the main road again, and travelled along it for a mile or more. Then he turned off once again. The lanes criss-crossed bewilderingly, and signposts were few. Sandy pressed on hopefully, taking one turn after another, until he had to admit to himself that he was lost. He had claimed to know the area well, but he didn't know where he was. He headed in what he thought was the general direction that he should take, and suddenly found himself approaching a familiar sign. He had seen that sign before, and just recently. The cottage and the angry gardener lay ahead. He slowed right down, and the van crawled apologetically up to the gardener, who took one belligerent look, then strode to the cottage door, and opening it, whistled. Sandy wound the window down, ready to make an abject apology, then he gasped, and the hairs on his neck rose as two animals appeared out of the cottage. If the name dog is applied correctly to those animals that are used by shepherds and police forces, then some other name should be coined for the creatures that Sandy now saw. Huge and shapeless and shaggy they were, and with teeth that would make a smiling alligator look positively gummy. They roared when they saw him, and rushed towards him and the van with terrible intent. Sandy grabbed the handle, and tried to close the window again, but he was far too hasty. Vans of that age have to be coaxed, not bullied. The handle came away in his hand, leaving the window wide open, and Sandy unprotected. The van, which was trembling as violently as he was, responded at once to his frantic foot, and they sped off down the lane, with the two hounds of hell in hot pursuit.

While Sandy was having problems with his deliveries, I was too busy in the shop to spare him even a passing thought. I was having small problems of my own, especially with the older customers, some of whom required all the tact that I could muster, and more besides.

Twig was a slightly built, wiry old man who had spent his working life on the land, and now in his retirement specialised in dowsing, or water divining He wore the same clothes all year round, whatever the weather, these being an old ex-army greatcoat, far too long for him, woollen mittens, with his fingers protruding, and a woollen balaclava hat of extreme age. On first sight I had mistaken Twig for a tramp, but had later found out that he was a resident of the next village, and was, in spite of appearances, meticulously clean. Twig had never travelled very far from home, and when he heard that Maggie and I came from Yorkshire, showed interest. "Whereabouts would Yorkshire be then, starting from here?" he enquired. "Oh, about two hundred miles or so to the north." I answered. Twig looked none the wiser. "Ah, that would be further than Cromer, I reckon." he said. "I ain't been to them parts yet, though I have a niece who lives up that way, married one o' your lot she did, for some reason." I thought it wiser not to reply, and Twig was also quiet for a while, then, "I did once go to Yarmouth with a friend." he said, almost defiantly. "Mind you," he added, "we did get lost on the road home."

On this occasion, Twig hung about until the shop was quiet before seeking my advice. "It's like this here," he said, pulling down the lower part of his balaclava so that I wouldn't miss a word. "That niece o'mine, the one I told you about, well, she reckons she's going to take me up to Yorkshire for a bit of a holiday." He looked round, and then whispered. "I don't want to go and make a fool of meself, not at my age, and in them foreign parts, so tell me, do they wear balaclavas in Yorkshire?"

Before I could answer the old man, a scornful cackle rang out through the shop. I recognised the sound. That voice could belong to no other than Granny Coster. I braced myself. "Call these things taters, do you?" she cried, stabbing at the vegetable display with her umbrella. "Well I've never seen such little lumpy old things in all my life. I'll bet they're some foreign muck. They ain't Norfolk grown." The young lady who happened to be standing near Granny gave me a smile. "No, Granny," she said. "They aren't potatoes at all. They're artichokes." "That they ain't," snapped the old lady. "Artichokes is all nice and leafy. I knows artichokes when I sees 'em. I ain't daft, you know." "Some artichokes are leafy," said the young woman, "But these are a different type. These are Jerusalem artichokes." "Jerusalem?" crowed Granny. "Jerusalem? There, what did I tell 'ee, I knew they weren't Norfolk grown." She gave the inoffensive vegetables another vicious jab with her brolly and then shuffled over to the counter. "Foreign rubbish," she called to them, over her shoulder.

I served Granny as quickly as I could, and then the young lady, feeling grateful for her sympathetic smile. I watched them leave, and heaved a sigh of relief, then went over to examine the artichokes for umbrella damage. I was lost in thought when the voice came, sounding rather hurt. "You didn't tell me," it said. It was Twig, still waiting patiently. "Do they, then?" he said. "Do they wear these here balaclavas up in Yorkshire?"

After Twig had left, Mrs. Larkin came into the shop. She was a customer who shopped with us regularly, and spent quite a large amount of money each week. She would come into the store and take up a basket and wander around the shelves, helping herself. When she had finished, she would hand me her shopping list, and I would go to the shelves and find the few oddments that she hadn't been able to find for herself. Each week there would be one item left on the list that was always the same. "Rice," the list said. At first, I had asked Mrs. Larkin whether this meant a packet of rice or a tin of rice. "Oh, it ain't rice at all," she had said. "It's spaghetti." I had taken the tin from the shelf, but had been surprised the next week when rice had been written down once again, and spaghetti required. After some time, I realised that Mrs. Larkin never did buy rice, though every week she did include it in her list, and every week she bought spaghetti.

I was packing her goods into her two voluminous shopping bags on this occasion, and making small talk as I did so, and I happened to mention the shopping list. "Tell me, Mrs. Larkin," I said, "why, if you know all the time that it's spaghetti that you require, do you put rice down on your list?" She didn't answer me at once. She paid for her goods and went as far as the door before she replied. "I always puts down rice on me list," she shouted at me, "'cos I can't spell spaghetti." She slammed the door violently as she left.

Sandy did eventually find his first call, after being out on the road for well over an hour. He was way behind time. He pulled himself together. He would make no more mistakes from now on. He put all memories of the gardener and his dogs out of his mind, and quite certain that he knew exactly where his second call was, set off smartly. He came to a fork in the road, and slowed down. That fork shouldn't be there, according to his memory. He was uncertain which way to go, and after wasting a couple of minutes thinking about it, he tossed a coin. When the coin fell heads up, he took the right hand lane. There was not a house or a building within sight, and very soon he had to admit to himself that he was lost once more. He was struck by something familiar in the shape of a tree that he had passed, and he slowed, a terrible sinking feeling in his stomach. Then the dreaded sign loomed up again, and he knew for certain just where he was. He stopped the van. He considered reversing, but dismissed the idea. It was a mile or so, and in reverse would take far too long. The gardener was still working away, ahead, but as yet hadn't seen the van. Sandy decided that he would have to race up to the cottage and turn round as quickly as was possible. With any luck he would be away before the man had time to call out his massive animals again. A few drops of rain fell, and he switched on the wipers. Then he braced himself for the charge. As the wipers swung, the horn sounded, and Sandy, now very tense, banged his head on the van roof as he jumped. The horn sounded again, then again. The gardener, hearing the sound, looked up from his labours, wondering who it was that was trying to attract his attention so insistently. When he saw the van, he threw down his spade with frightening force, and charged through the cottage door. "Mock me, would you," he snarled as he went. He reappeared with the two terrible dogs and a double-barrelled shotgun, which he loaded expertly as he walked.

Sandy hurtled towards the cottage, the old van shaking frantically as it went, then he skidded round in the fastest three point turn that the vehicle had ever executed in its long and chequered career. He spun the rear wheels in his haste to get away, and the two demon dogs gained a few yards on him. He whimpered as he saw them in the mirror, then controlling himself with an effort, was away, and moving faster than the dogs could run. They grew smaller in the mirror, and he was heaving a sigh of relief when suddenly the ignition cut out, and the engine faded. The van slowed, and the dogs gained. Sandy panicked. With such teeth as they

67

had, they could have ripped their way through the sides of the van to get at him. With his window jammed open, he was surely doomed. His foot was pressed down to the floor in his fear, but the van was still slowing. He whimpered again, then suddenly the fault righted itself. The engine picked up. The van leapt forward. The unburnt mixture in the exhaust ignited, and the backfire that followed was deafening. The two huge dogs, who were far more familiar with guns than with vans, immediately turned and raced for home, yelping with fear. The ill-tempered gardener, hearing the report, and seeing the dogs hurtling towards him, came to the natural conclusion. "Blarst me, he's shooting at my dogs," he roared, and raising his gun to his shoulder, he loosed off both barrels at the departing van. The rattling old vehicle was almost out of range, but not quite, and the sound of the shot bouncing off the metalwork didn't do Sandy's shattered nerves any good at all. He headed back towards the shop, flat out. Behind him, the gardener stood in the lane and spoke to his dogs. "I reckon that's the last we'll see of him, lads," he said. "That'll teach them city types to come out into the country and dump their scrap cars on us."

Sandy should have been back at the shop at around two o'clock. When three came and there was no sign of him, we began to be slightly worried. At four we were looking anxiously down the road, and at five Maggie had convinced herself that the van had broken down somewhere out in the wilds. At six she was certain that it had developed some fatal fault, and crashed, killing poor young Sandy outright. The fault was mine, for buying an old wreck of a van that was obviously a death trap.

When Sandy did arrive, quite unharmed, it was past six thirty, and we had closed up the shop. Sandy said that he hadn't delivered most of the orders, and made it absolutely clear that nothing in the world would persuade him to do so. He wished to give notice, right there on the spot, and leave at once. There was nothing else that I could do but leave my tea and set off and deliver the goods myself. Not claiming Sandy's expert knowledge of the area, I took an Ordnance Survey map with me, and had very little trouble finding the calls, but it was still very late when I got back, and I had a few very rude remarks to make about the delivery service. Maggie agreed with me that the scheme had been a failure, and the whole idea should be dropped. "But you'll be stuck with that old wreck of a van," she said. "I still say it's not worth any more then ten pounds. You'll never get your money back."

The next morning, I was taking down the notice in the shop when the very same farmer who had coveted the old van came in. Here was the chance for me to cut my losses, I told myself. If I could only unload the old van onto him, things wouldn't have turned out too badly, after all. "Good morning, you're just the very man that I was hoping to see," I said to him. "That van of mine, the one that you said that you liked so much. I'm thinking of selling it, and if you're still interested, you can have first chance. I'll show you the receipt, and you can have it for exactly the same price that I paid for it, a week ago." "Well, that sounds like a very fair deal to me," said the farmer. I shot a knowing smile in Maggie's direction, and she raised her eyes to the ceiling. "How much did you give for it then? A fiver?" asked the farmer. I reeled. "You must be joking," I said. "That's a pretty rare vehicle. You told me yourself that there weren't very many of that model about." The farmer nodded. "Yes," he said. "I did say something like that, but I didn't mean that it was a particularly rare model. I just meant that there aren't many old bangers about in these parts that are in such a bad state that a farmer can pick one up for a fiver or so, and use it as a chicken coop." I turned and left the shop, avoiding Maggie's eyes as I did so.

CHAPTER FIVE.

THE NELSON TOUCH.

The large bottle green van with the old fashioned gold lettering on its sides stood in the village street and glowed in the morning sun. Its paintwork shone, its brass radiator glistened, its wire wheels sparkled. With the background of flint cottages and thatched roofs it looked like some colourful mirage from a previous age, although never in its long life, even when it had been new, had the van looked quite as immaculate as it did now. It was an old tradesman's van, one of a beautifully restored and preserved collection that was housed in what used to be the stable block of the old hall. By the side of the magnificent vehicle, nonchalantly proud in a green and gold uniform of the same era, stood Percy, the ex-military man and surely the smartest of the village's many pensioners. Ben, another pensioner of around Percy's age, came weaving his way along the street, ragged and stubbled, and waving his stick. He stopped in mid-grumble, when his eyes lighted on his

71

friend, and the splendid van, and a look of wonder came over his face. "Gaw," he said, and walked slowly around the van, reaching out a calloused hand and touching the paintwork reverently now and then. "Law," he said, and walked equally slowly around his friend, pausing to finger the material of the lapels in awe. Percy tried hard, but he couldn't prevent his chest from swelling, ever so slightly, sending his row of medals bobbing.

"What's all this about then?" demanded Ben. "What the devil's going on?" "The old van's taking part in the agricultural show today," said Percy, in a casual manner that suggested that he was already quite bored with the whole thing. "I've got the job of driving it out there, parading it around the ring a few times, you know the kind of thing, and then bringing it back again." If green is the colour of envy, then Ben should by rights have turned the colour of Percy's uniform. He slapped his stick against his trouser leg, and barked. "This is the first I've heard about all this. Why didn't folk know about it in the pub, long ago?" Percy's face adopted an expression that Ben had never seen before, except once, on a photograph of a camel that had claimed his place in history by siring a record number of offspring. "We at the Hall," he said, "don't usually discuss our social engagements in the village pub." Ben scratched his stubble noisily. "I'm older than you," he said, trying not to sound too jealous of his friend. "I should have been picked to drive an old van like this." "But you've never driven anything except a farm tractor," said Percy. "You haven't even got a licence, have you?" Ben grunted. "I still say it ain't fair," he said. "And I wouldn't have needed to have a road licence just to drive it round the ring. We could have shared." "I think you're just jealous," said Percy, with a half smile. "You fancy yourself in this uniform, I suppose, and you'd like to see your photo in all the papers, like mine's going to be, but a uniform wouldn't suit you at all. You ain't used to wearing one, not like me." Ben slapped his stick against his ragged trouser leg again in temper. "It ain't that at all," he snapped. "I'm not the sort who gets mad at somebody else's good luck, and if I was you, I wouldn't get too uppetty about this job. That ain't like you at all. Before you gets carried away with it all, just remember that this blarsted show is only on for today, and you've still got to live with the rest of us afterwards." Percy flicked an invisible fleck of dust from his bottle green sleeve, and stifled a yawn. "I won't," he said. "You might, if you was in my position, but I won't. I'm used to parades and things, and being the centre of attention." Ben grated his teeth and banged his stick against his leg again, this time with more force, and his eyes went suddenly watery as he caught his ankle bone.

"Morning," said a voice, and P.C. Danby, the village policeman strolled up. For once, he was out of uniform, for today he was off duty, and he too was going to the show. His glance took in the van, and the uniformed driver, and his lips pursed in a complimentary whistle. Percy strutted, ever so slightly. "My word," said Danby. "That's a neat old turn-out, and no mistake." He gave the van a cursory inspection. "Well done," he said. "Mind you, that offside rear tyre is just about ready for changing. Another few miles and it will be dangerous." Percy spoke, with the newly-found arrogance that he had donned with the uniform. "I assume from your style of dress, that you are not on duty, constable." he said. Danby blinked. He hadn't been called constable by a villager for years, and never, if his memory served him right, by old Percy. "And as you are obviously out to enjoy yourself today," went on Percy. "Might I suggest that you mind your own business, and let other people do the same." Ben stopped rubbing his ankle bone, and grinned in expectation, looking eagerly at Danby. Danby's face set, and his hand moved automatically to the place where his breast pocket would have been, had he been on duty. Then he stopped, and looked thoughtfully at Percy. He could have told the pensioner that a good policeman was never off duty, but he didn't. "Right you are, Percy," he said. "I'll do just that. I'll mind my own business. I'll turn a blind eye on you, just for today, but tomorrow, when the show's over, and I'm back in uniform, and you are out of yours, we'll see." Ben gave a snort of disappointment. Percy didn't answer. He adjusted his peaked cap in the mirror-bright paintwork of the van, then climbed up into the driving seat with great dignity.

Ben and P.C. Danby were driven to the show by Jack, the village's jobbing builder. Jack's van was also an old one, but there the resemblance to Percy's vehicle ended. Instead of being polished and serviced, Jack's van had been regularly overloaded and under-serviced, and equally regularly abused and ill-treated for the whole of its working life. Like a tinker's dog, though, the van always tried to please its hard master, and it did its best; though its best was very often a sluggish walking pace, especially uphill. Percy's magnificent specimen was in a different class altogether, and this point was rubbed home with some force when the three were about half-way along their journey, and the beautiful green and gold vehicle overtook them. It scudded past them on a dangerous bend, cutting in front so that Jack had to brake and swerve in order to keep his van on the road. "You should do him for that, Danby," said Ben, crouched in the back amongst a tangle of tools and enraged by the sight of Percy, upright and aloof in the open cab, complete with goggles and gauntlets. "No," said Danby. "You heard what I told him back there. This is my day off, so I'm turning a blind eye on him, but don't you worry, pride goes before a fall."

The three forgot all about Percy and the green van for a while, once they had joined the milling crowd at the showground. There were old friends to be greeted, and new farm machinery to be inspected, and side shows and exhibitions to be seen, and then there were pork pies and pints of beer for lunch. After that there were the ring events, and the highlight was the parade of tradesmen's vehicles of yesteryear. The green van was the star of the show, and Ben stood and watched with grudging admiration as Percy headed the parade, while the spectators applauded, and the photographers angled to get a shot of the van that showed the driver, so perfectly in keeping, with his green and gold uniform, peaked cap, gauntlets and goggles.

After that, they wandered around the side shows once more, and Ben was so much out of sorts with himself, that he even paid money to have his fortune told, crossing the Original Gipsy Daisy Dee's palm with hard earned silver only to be told that he was too easy going where money was concerned. The three headed for the beer tent, and settling themselves comfortably, prepared to get down to some serious drinking before the journey home. Danby seemed to be as relaxed as the other two, but although he did join in the general chatter, his gaze every now and then went to the mirror that was hanging in the central pole of the tent, through which he could see, over the grass, the old green van.

The next time Ben saw his estranged friend Percy was when he too came into the beer tent. He noticed that he had discarded his uniform jacket in the sweltering heat, and was relaxing in his shirtsleeves. Ben didn't speak to Percy, but looked across the grass to where the van was standing. Then, with nothing particular in mind, he left the tent, and wandered across, drawn by the magnetic beauty of the old vehicle. He paused and looked at the green jacket, lying folded on the grass, with its gold piping glowing. He looked round. No-one was watching, in fact no-one was anywhere near him. He slipped out of his own ragged tweed, and quickly donned the green. Then he slowly walked round the van, stroking it, and fondly murmuring compliments. He climbed up into the cab, and touching the controls one by one, daydreamed for a few moments. It really would have been an experience to have driven such a vehicle, and experiences such as that didn't come round very often in his life. And he would have had the photographs, too. He could always have looked at them later, and remembered.

He was roused from his reverie by a coarse voice shouting in his ear. "I see by the name on the side that this old bus is going back to the next village to ours." Ben turned, and saw that the speaker was a tall and weatherbeaten young farmer. "We've had a spot of trouble with the old lorry that we came in and it won't get us home." said the man. "That's bad luck," said Ben, climbing down from the van with reluctance. "Well, do you reckon it would be worth a pound to get a lift back in this?" said the farmer. Ben scratched at his stubble. His mind was still on the old van. "When you're in a fix like you are, it must be worth two," he said, trying to make out his reflection in the paintwork. "Why, you greedy little grasper," said the farmer, then he roared with laughter, sending gusts of beer-laden breath over Ben. "All right then, you win, here you are." He pushed two pound notes into Ben's hand, and opening the back door of the van, climbed in. "Hey, wait a minute," shouted Ben, coming out of his daydream, but a second hand proffered another two pounds, and he stopped, and stared at the money. "What is it?" asked the first man from the depths of the van. "Oh, er," said Ben, thinking rapidly. "It's just that once you're in, I'll have to close the back door on you, and it'll be just like sitting in a big biscuit tin. You can't let yourself out of there, 'cos there ain't no handle on the inside." "Righto, my little green gremlin." laughed the farmer. "You just drive carefully, that's all. Remember there's no padding in here, and nothing to sit on but the floor." Ben stood in silence, and more money was thrust upon him as more farmers climbed into the van. When the last one had climbed aboard, Ben had twenty pounds in his hand. He closed the van door on the farmers, his hands trembling.

Ben stuffed the money into his trouser pocket, hardly daring to believe his luck. He looked round furtively. No, he hadn't been seen, no-one was watching. He didn't see the mirror, across the grass, in the beer tent, or the reflection in it of Danby's eyes. "Gaw, wait till Percy comes back to his van," he chortled. "If he keeps that drunken lot locked up in there for long they'll murder him when he lets 'em out." He paused in his efforts to unbutton the jacket, and bent over for a second, shaking with laughter. Then he took a deep breath, and wiping his eyes, prepared to discard the green jacket and make his escape. A heavy hand descended suddenly on his shoulder, and stifling a yell with difficulty, he turned. He found himself looking up into the eyes of a uniformed policeman.

"Move it," said the constable, without smiling. "Move it, it shouldn't be here." Ben swallowed. "Er, but...." he said. "No buts, move it..." said the policeman, even more emphatically. "Shift that van. The tractors have to come through here in a few minutes, and you're blocking the way." "Ah," said Ben. He didn't move. "Do you want to argue with me?" said the policeman, bending until his face was uncomfortably close to Ben's. "Do you want to have to show me all your documents? Should I have a really good look around that van of yours, at the tyres, say? Or are you going to be sensible, and get in that cab and move it?" Ben gulped again, and then nodded. "I'll move it," he said.

Percy had been quite right when he had said earlier that Ben had never driven anything other than a farm tractor, and that he didn't hold a licence. He had certainly never in his life driven a vehicle that had controls that looked anything like those that he was going to have to manipulate now. His hands trembled as he fumbled with the unfamiliar vehicle under the stern and steady gaze of the law. The laughter of a few minutes ago was already forgotten, and his mind was racing as he gave the constable a sickly smile and then gulped. If he admitted to the policeman that he didn't know how to drive the van, and that he didn't have a licence, how could he explain the green jacket, and what charges would be brought against him in court? And what about the men in the back? He would be jailed, surely, for taking all that money from the farmers. No. He had no option. He had to drive the van, even if only for a few yards, just to satisfy the policeman, then he could make his getaway.

Ben managed to start the engine, and then fiddled with the large floor mounted gearstick. He chewed bits off the gears for a while, as the policeman watched him with raised eyebrows. Ben could see Percy, standing far away in the beer tent, his braces dangling and a pint of beer in his hand. Percy didn't look round. Ben wrenched the gearstick about desperately, until it fell into a well worn groove. Then, revving the old engine violently, he let in the clutch. The van leapt forward, and Ben gasped. His old farm tractor never behaved in such reckless fashion. The policeman gave a shake of his head as the van began to move, and then turned away to steal a quiet smoke behind one of the tents. Across the grass, Danby nodded to himself as he gazed at the mirror.

Ben very quickly discovered that the tyres of the old

van didn't grip on the damp grass nearly as well as the tyres of a farm tractor did. The van kept tending to slide sideways, and his attempts to correct this merely led to the vehicle progressing in a zig-zag manner instead of a straight line. The degree of control that he had over the steering was minimal, and although he did just manage to miss the St. John Ambulance tent by a whisker, incidentally curing a teenager of a distressing attack of hiccups as he did so, he didn't miss the next one.

The Original Gipsy Daisy Dee was gravely assuring a paunchy middle aged man about the romantic future that lay ahead of him when the great green van burst in on their little occult world. "You are going to make a sudden and unexpected move," she stated, her raven locks swinging heavily. "And that will cause great excitement in your life. I can see it clearly." The man quivered at the thought of the forthcoming excitement, and his red neck bulged over his collar. "Go on, my dear, go on," he said, his outstretched palm sweating. "You will take a short trip," said the gipsy. "And after that, nothing will ever be quite the same again." The side wall of the canvas tent suddenly took on the shape and movement of an advancing Centurion tank. The tank demolished the gipsy's table in its attack, and the table pushed the man, with irresistible force. He was flung several feet through the opening of the tent, landing on his back a mere split second before the Original Gipsy Daisy Dee arrived, heavily, on top of him. Her raven locks had now flown away like the blackbird, and a platinum blonde frizz showed over a face whose deep tan ended at what used to be the hairline of her wig.

Behind them, the van roared on its way, its windscreen now covered with the flapping canvas of the tent. With all forward visibility gone, Ben knocked the van out of gear and stood on the brake. There was no response, and his next thought was to leap out of the cab, but they were moving too fast for that. They were rolling down some kind of slope; though the wheels of the van were locked, they seemed to be sliding along on mud.

In the darkness of the back of the van, the farmers were flung into a heap at the rear when the van first set off. They had just managed to sort themselves out when they were flung into a heap at the front, as Ben tried to stop. The darkness didn't help their humour, nor did the beer that they had recently consumed. The van slid on down the slope, and the sound of running water came to Ben's frightened ears. He looked to the side,

as he couldn't see anything ahead, and he saw water, pretty deep water, so deep that it came up over the floor of the cab. He sniffed the air, trying to smell salt, and tried to remember how far the showground was from the coast. In his consternation at the sight of the water, he instinctively lifted his foot from the brake. The farmers, in the back, didn't hear the water, and they didn't see it, but they felt it, as they were flung about the floor, and the van was filled with terrible promises of what they were intending to do to a certain little green gremlin, if they were fortunate enough to survive the trip home.

The van began to roll uphill, and out of the water. Ben sighed with relief. He ought to have known, he told himself. The gipsy never mentioned a word about a trip by sea. The uphill motion soon slowed and the van ran gently backwards. As it did so, the canvas fell from the windscreen, and Ben saw exactly where he was. He was in the middle of the broad shallow stream that ran across the edge of the showground. He realised also that now the van was in that position, there was no way that it would ever be able to get out under its own power. The muddy bank was far too steep and slippery for that. It would need a tractor to pull it free. A good old farm tractor, he told himself, just like the one that he was used to driving.

The sound of bumping and swearing from the rear told him that although the van was at rest, the gang of farmers was still on the move. He shuddered at the thought of what they might do to him if they managed to get free. He must get away, and quickly. The van had settled heavily on the bed of the stream now, and the waterlogged engine had given one final shudder and died. Ben jumped out, into a couple of feet of water, and waded to the bank. He gave one last panic-stricken look towards the van. Was it his imagination, or were the walls actually bulging? Then he ran across the grass towards the beer tent and his friends. As he passed the place where he had left his jacket, he slipped out of the green tunic while still on the move, and dropping it roughly where he had found it, grabbed up his own grubby garment and ran on. His pace slowed as he neared the beer tent, and his panic died, and his sense of humour returned. By the time he reached his friends and regained his seat, he was once again gasping for breath as he tried to stifle his mirth. "Oh Gaw, Oh Law," he muttered. "Wait till old Percy goes back to his van." Danby noticed his amusement, and his wet legs, but said nothing.

Turning round, Percy glanced idly in the direction of his van, then he choked on his beer. The van was gone. It must have been stolen. He left his drink and ran across the grass. His jacket was still there. He snatched it up and pulled it on as he looked round. There was water and mud on the lower part of the garment, and he brushed at it hastily. Someone had been messing about with it. He would have to clean it up before he took it back to the hall. Concern about the jacket was driven from his mind when he caught sight of the van. It was down at the bottom of a slope, and was standing in a shallow stream. "Oh, no." he groaned. "The handbrake. I must have forgotten to put it on." He caught sight of the Original Gipsy Daisy Dee, sitting by what looked like a pile of firewood, and apparently having hysterics. She was being consoled by a group of ladies in nurses uniform, and a portly man wearing a light grey suit with a bright green skid mark right up the back. "I can't understand it, my dear," the man was saying. "Surely, you should have seen it coming." The gipsy answered him with another scream. Percy saw the tyre marks, and groaned again. He could be in serious trouble for allowing his runaway van to cause such damage. A uniformed policeman strolled by, looking the other way, and Percy turned away quickly. He wanted no trouble with the law.

He strolled towards the van, trying to look casual, as if he regularly parked it in mid-stream. He stopped at the waters edge, and tried to assess the condition of the vehicle. Apart from splashes of mud, the van seemed to be unharmed. Steam rose from the engine, but Percy had dried out many a wet engine in his time, and the thought of doing it again didn't worry him. He could get one of his farming friends to tow the van out with a tractor, and then all would be well. A good clean up, and he could forget that the accident had ever happened. Then he heard noises, and they seemed to be coming from the back of the van. "That must be kids," he snarled. "That's what happened. They messed up my jacket, and then they started to fool about with my van." His anger increased as he thought of the juveniles. "It was probably them who took off the brake, and not my fault at all," he said. "And even if it wasn't them, I'll blame 'em, if I can just get my hands on one or two of 'em." He waded into the water, and flung the back door of the van open, shouting as he did so. "Right, you young beggars. You think you can do just as you like, don't you? Well I'm going to show you a thing or two." "Oh, you are, are you?" said a deep voice, and a large, wet, and hairy arm reached out, and gripping him by the collar, lifted him clean off his feet.

In the beer tent, the three companions had drunk as much as they considered wise, at such a distance from home. They were ready to leave. They climbed into the van, and Jack drove carefully across the grass towards the exit. Glancing to one side as they went, he saw the green van standing in the stream, and the strange scene that was being enacted nearby. He brought the van to a halt, and the three watched the activity with interest for a while. A gang of large, brown-skinned men had Percy, and were obviously holding him prisoner. Four of them had him firmly in their grasp, and upside down, his head only a few inches from the water. "Hey, Danby," said Jack, with genuine alarm. "Do something. They're going to drown him." Danby settled himself comfortably as he watched. "Oh, I don't think so," he said. "I know all those fellers personally, and there isn't a villain amongst 'em. Mind you, I don't suppose Percy knows that." "You know, for a little chap like he is, Percy's got a terrible loud voice, ain't he." said Ben, failing to keep the chuckle out of his voice. Percy's yell came to them very clearly. "I tell you it wasn't me," he bawled. "Oh, no?" said the chief of his tormentors. "And just how many little green gremlins like you do you think there are, running around this place? Give us our money back." "I tell you I can't," roared Percy. "I haven't got it." "Well you'd better tell us where you've hidden it." said the farmer. "Right lads, give him a dip." They dunked the head of the little green figure like a doughnut in the water. When it emerged, the green one's hair was pointed up on the top of its head, like the wick on a candle. "Where's our money?" demanded the farmer again. The green and muddy one only gurgled. "Oh, Gaw," chortled Ben. "Don't he look different now to what he did when he passed us on the road?" "You'll have to do something, Danby," said Jack. "That's a crime that's being committed. It's blackmail, isn't it?" "No. Extortion, maybe." said the policeman, without concern. "Or money with menaces perhaps?" He grinned. "But I see no signal." "Signal?" said Ben, looking puzzled. "What do you mean, signal?" "Nelson," said Danby. "Turning a blind eye, and all that stuff." "But Nelson did say that every man should do his duty," said Jack. "And you're a policeman, and you know what your duty should be." Danby grinned again. "Ah, but I'm not on

84

duty, am I?" he said, "Remember what I told Percy this morning."

They watched the group in the stream again for a few seconds in silence. Then Jack looked at Danby. "Well, what are you going to do?" he asked. "I'll tell you what we're all going to do," said the policeman. "We're going to round off a good day with one last drink. You drive us back to the village, and we'll call and have a last one at George's place." "Not me," said Jack. "I reckon I've spent about as much as I can afford today." "Oh, don't you worry about that side of things," said Danby. "I'm quite certain that Ben here will be able to put his hands on a bit of spare cash, and will be only too pleased to treat us both, won't you, Ben?" He gave Ben a long hard look, and the expression of satisfaction on the old man's face was replaced by one of apprehension. "But it'll be long after closing time when we get there." he quavered. Danby closed one eye. "Never mind about that," he said. "George will serve you all right, I mean, he always does, doesn't he? And as I'm still off duty, I'll turn my blind eye."

CHAPTER SIX.

THE ICE BREAKER.

When Dr. John left the village, his going was regarded as a catastrophe by most of the locals. He had looked after them so well, and for so many years, and knew each family and their individual ailments so intimately that the villagers were quite certain that there would never be another doctor fit to take his place. This attitude was very hard on Dr. Hapton, who was to be our new G.P. He was a fine doctor, and a true Christian, as we were to learn later, but it did take the village quite a few weeks to accept him.

"Good morning. My name is Doctor Hapton; I'm your new doctor," he said, the first time that Maggie and I met him. "I wonder if you would display this small notice in your window for me. You see, I've been here all week, and I haven't had a single patient yet." He handed me a small notice about the size of a postcard. "I think that many of the older villagers might be under the impression that the surgery has closed down altogether, now that Dr. John has left," he said. "I just want everyone to know that things are to continue as normal, and that they can come and see me just as they used to go to Dr. John." "Well, they will be very cautious at first," I said. "We found that, when we first came to the village. That's just the way they are. But once you've dealt with a couple of them, the word will get round that you're quite human, and then you'll probably find that you're busier than you really want to be." The doctor sighed. "I can't wait," he said, "I know that I expected things to be a little slower in the country, but this is dreadful. In my last practice, I would look down at least a hundred throats a day, and get them to say Aaah. Since I've been here though, the only throat that I've looked down has been that of Dolly Foster, and she's my nurse and receptionist." Maggie smiled and nodded. Dolly was engaged to John, Old Ben's clumsy son, and she would have been soft-hearted enough to invent a symptom or two, if the new doctor had been feeling depressed by the lack of patients. "Don't you worry, doctor," she said. "The locals will soon get over your newness, then you'll be busy." "I hope you're right," said the doctor. "But at the moment, an outbreak of tonsillitis and a couple of dozen Aaahs, would cheer me up no end." "Ah," I said, sympathetically, and the new doctor looked at me sharply. "I'm sorry," I said. "I didn't mean to be funny."

I placed the doctor's notice in a prominent position in the window, and Maggie and I brought his name up in conversation with the customers as often as we could, but the villagers still stayed away from the surgery in droves.

Maggie had a word with Dolly Foster about the situation. "Can't you persuade a couple of the older folk to go and see him?" she said, "just to get the ball rolling. All the others will join in then. They're all curious really, they just don't want to be the first to go, that's all." "Well,

I'll have to do something like that," said Dolly. "If things go on like this for much longer, I can see myself being out of a job." "How about Old Ben?" said Maggie. "You know him well enough to talk to him. If he went to the surgery, all the other pensioners would follow suit." Dolly gave the matter some thought. "He's a stubborn old so-and-so," she said. "He's got plenty of minor ailments, but nothing major. I've never known him to visit a doctor. Still, I wonder if I could work on him a bit, and make a small mountain out of one of his tiny little molehills, without scaring him to death." "It might be worth a try." said Maggie, and the two of them got their heads together.

When Ben complained, as he regularly did, about his lumbago, his son John took no notice of him at all. Having heard Ben complaining in a similar fashion all his life, he accepted the grumbling as being part of Ben's nature, and normal. His own massively strong frame had so seldom felt a twinge of pain of any kind that sympathy didn't come readily to him.

When John's girl friend Dolly heard the old man complaining, she suddenly expressed a sympathy and interest that the old man had never known, and he spent many long minutes relating his medical history to her. He explained why he hadn't been to a doctor about his complaint for years. "They can't do anything for me except give me them pain-killing tablets," he said. "And I don't like taking the things. They send me a bit funny in the head." He ignored a snort from John, and went on. "In any case, I can't have me pint o' beer of a night when I'm on 'em, and that's enough to make me feel bad, apart from the backache." "But doctors can do a lot of things today that they couldn't do a few years ago." said Dolly. "There are all kinds of new drugs and treatments. This new doctor that we've got is really up to date. Why don't you let me take you along to see him?"

Ben shook his head. "If I could only get me hands on some of the good old fashioned rubbin' liquor, and get somebody to rub it in for me, I reckon I'd be fine," he said. "The doctor can prescribe something just as good." said Dolly. "No," said Ben, doggedly. "It ain't the same." Dolly pouted. "You're a very stubborn old man," she said. "But I'll make a bargain with you. If I get hold of some of that old fashioned liniment, and rub it into your back, will you promise to come to the doctor's surgery if it doesn't cure you?" "It'll work if you rubs it in right," said Ben. "Well, I am a nurse," said Dolly. "I'll do it correctly, now, is that a bargain?" "It is," said Ben. "But you'll never get the stuff."

"I'm ashamed of you," said Dolly to John. "Your own father, suffering in this way, and you doing nothing at all about it." "I've done everything that I can," protested John. "I even offered to buy him a hot water bottle for his back, that time when the Post Office was selling 'em off cheap, in the middle of last summer, but he said that they were just for old folk, and he wouldn't have one." "You've never tried rubbing his back with liniment though, have you?" Dolly accused. "He told me so himself. He has to buy that stuff at the Post Office and then try to rub it into his back himself. It just can't be done. Somebody else has to rub it in properly." John shuddered, and shook his head. "If you knew him as well as I do, you wouldn't want to rub anything into his back, or anywhere else. I'd sooner kill and draw a couple of geese, any time. Anyway, he says that stuff's no good; he reckons it isn't as strong as the old stuff used to be." "Well, why not try to get some of the old stuff?" Dolly persisted. "You get it and I'll rub it into his back for him." John looked surly, but didn't answer. "There must be other people in the village who have had the same trouble," said Dolly. "And I'll bet there are bottles of the old stuff standing about on shelves all over the place.

89

Just ask, that's all I'm saying. Just ask." "All right, all right," said John. "I'll ask around, if you say so." "I do," said Dolly. "And don't you forget it."

John spent a good part of his lunch hour talking to the older members of the community, trying to find out if any of them had ever suffered from lumbago, and used the old liniment. "Young 'Enry used to get it from time to time." said Percy, the pensioner, as he straightened his back from his gardening. "I don't think he gets it now, but he used to." "Thanks," said John, and headed for 'Enry's farm. 'Enry was just about to set off in his car when John caught up with him, panting. "Hey, before you go," he said. "Can you let me have a drop of your old liniment, if you've got any about?" "Can't it wait?" said 'Enry, looking at the clock on the village church. "I'm in a hurry." "No, it can't," said John. "I promised, and if I don't get some today, Dolly will mob me something terrible tonight." "Well, if it's as urgent as all that," said 'Enry reluctantly, getting out of his car, and he went into the farmhouse. He came out and handed John a bottle containing about half a pint of cloudy liquid. "Now I'll have to go," he said. "I'm late already." "Here," shouted John. "What do I owe you?" "Oh, buy me a pint some time," called 'Enry, as he roared away.

In the cottage that night, having been informed of the existence of the old rubbing liquor, Ben prepared himself for treatment before supper. He had had a bath for the occasion, even though, as he said to John, he hadn't done anything for months to get himself dirty. He'd put on a clean shirt, clean socks, and a pair of trousers which, as he commented, "might not be clean, but are at least different, not bein' warmed up yet."

When Dolly arrived, Ben laid himself face down the the sofa, his head on a cushion. "Well, here we go, let's see what the old fashioned stuff can do," said Dolly, pulling up his shirt tail. "'Ere, 'ang on a bit," said Ben, pulling it down again. "No need to strip me. I don't want ter get new monia. Draughts is bad for backs." "Now don't be silly," said Dolly firmly. "It's the small of your back I'm trying to uncover, nothing else." Ben grunted, and adjusted his clothing so that he laid bare the minimum amount of flesh necessary for the completion of the operation. John stared at the bared area, and a shudder ran through his strong frame. "Gaw, look at it," he said in disgust. "It's all hairy and patchy. If a pig looked like that, it would be condemned as unfit for eating. Gaw, look at all them horrible hairs." "Well, what do you expect on a fellow's back? Feathers?" snapped Ben. Dolly smiled and shook her head. "Now stop it, the two of you," she said. "Lie still, I'm going to start, and this stuff is too precious to waste, so don't make me spill any of it." She poured a little of the liniment into her hand, and applied it to the affected part. "Ah, that's better." said Ben after only a few seconds. "Oh that's gettin' to the heart of it all right. Put some more on, gel." Dolly splashed a liberal amount of the liquid onto his back, and with a gurgle from the bottle, filled her cupped hand again. Ben smiled through his stubble. "Ah," he said dreamily. "It's enough to send you off to sleep. It's all sort of warm and comfortable like. It's real good stuff, like I told you." "Well, it might work," said Dolly. "This might be just what you've been needing." She applied even more of the lotion. "If you can get a couple of good nights sleep, you might be able to shake the lumbago off altogether, but remember, if it doesn't go, then it's off with me to the doctors." Dolly didn't notice as she spoke that some of the liniment was running down Ben's back and disappearing.

"Yes," said the old man drowsily. "But I think I'm goin' to be all right. I think—." He stopped talking, and his old frame quivered. His head shot up from the cushion, his eyes now wide open, and staring. "Eeeow!" he yelled, and with a burst of energy that was astonishing for one of his years, leapt from the sofa, landing in an upright position at one bound. "Oh Gaw, Oh Law, Oh help!" he bawled, and brushing his astonished son aside, he shot out of the room and into the kitchen. Whatever it was that he was looking for in there, he evidently didn't find it, and didn't waste too much time searching for it, for he was back in the room again in a split second. "Eeeow!" he yelled again, and charged round the room at an incredible speed. "I didn't think that the stuff would work in that way," said John, watching his speeding father with wonder. "It shouldn't do," said Dolly. "Something's gone wrong." "Perhaps he's gone off his head with the pain," said John. "I always told you he was a bit funny in the head, didn't I?" Dolly shielded her eyes from the scene with her hands. "Never mind all the talking." she said. "Get some trousers on him. It isn't decent." "Yaaaah!" shouted Ben, still travelling at a rapid rate. He paused for a fraction of a split second to rub his hind parts on the door frame, and then, obviously discovering that this exercise didn't bring him the relief that he sought, set off round the room again. "I'd best slip the bolt on the door," said John. "Else he'll be off round the village." He dodged the speeding figure with a hasty sidestep, and went to the door.

It was fortunate for the caller that he chose that particular moment to knock. At any other time that evening, he would have had difficulty making himself heard above Ben's yelling voice and thudding feet. John opened the door, and looked sourly at the man who stood there. The man wore a serious expression, and was holding out his hand as if for John to shake it. His lapel was hidden behind a large and colourful rosette, and election forms and leaflets were sticking out of his side pockets. John ignored the outstretched hand and looked critically at the stranger. "I wished to have a quick word with the gentlemen who live here," said the man, staring past John with a fixed gaze. "We ain't got no gentlemen here," said John. "Only me and him." The man passed his hand over his eyes and looked past John again. The room was not particularly well lit, but he could make out the figure of a young woman, quite respectable in appearance, and the whisky bottle that she was holding. The other figure in the room was moving about just a little too rapidly for him to be sure what it was, but it seemed to be male, and was wearing nothing but a shirt, and long, old fashioned underwear. It was travelling round the room at a very high speed, and high-stepping it over the occasional piece of furniture as it went. From time to time it uttered a weird sort of animal noise. "What party are you with then?" asked John, seeing the rosette and leaflets. "Oh I'm not one for going to parties, really," said the man hurriedly. "But please, don't let me interrupt yours. I'm sorry I intruded." He backed away, still holding out his hand, but this time as though to ward off some danger.

John turned back to the room, and was just in time to see Ben hurtle off upstairs. John had hardly got his foot on the first stair, to follow him, when the old man passed him again, on the way down. "Get it orf," he yelled in despair as he went past. "Give me something to get it orf." "I didn't think I'd ever see you move as quick as that," said John thoughtfully. "It must be doing you a power of good, this morning you could hardly walk." "Aaaoo!" screamed the old man, and as he passed his son this time, he brought him a heavy clout round the ear. "Get it orf!" he bawled, and disappeared upstairs again. Dolly ran into the kitchen, and came back with a towel, soaked in cold water. "Here," she said to John, holding it out with her head turned away. "Give him this." Ben burst down the stairs again, and snatched the towel from her hand with a frantic motion. He tore round the room once more, wrapping the towel around himself like a loin cloth as he went, and then he disappeared into the kitchen at a fast gallop.

John and Dolly stood looking at each other and listening. The noises that came from the kitchen gradually subsided from yelling and bumping to creaking and moaning. At last John stuck his head round the door. He found Ben crouched in a chair, his trousers pulled on over the wet towel, which he was wearing as a baby wears a nappie. He was rocking to and fro, and moaning softly to himself.

"You're walking a lot better today," said John to his father the next morning in the Post Office. Ben didn't answer him. Dolly too was unusually quiet as she paid for her purchases. "Did that old liniment do the trick then, John?" came 'Enry's voice from the doorway. "How is the horse?" John looked at the speaker, open mouthed. "We, er, I mean, he," he said, pointing to Ben, "had a little bit of trouble with it." "A little bit," said Ben savagely, gripping his stick tightly, and glaring at his son. "Well I can't understand that," said 'Enry. "It's darn good stuff, my old father used it for years, it's made up to his own secret recipe, you know. I've never known it to fail. You didn't get it in your eyes or anything, did you?" "No," snarled Ben. "I didn't get it in my eyes." "Well, it always got 'em going," said 'Enry, puzzled. "Oh, it got him going all right," said John, edging a stick's length away from his father. "I think he could have won the Grand National at the rate he was going."

"You will come along to the surgery now, and get some proper treatment, won't you?" said Dolly. "That I won't," said Ben, gritting his teeth. "But you promised," said Dolly. "That was before," said Ben. "If last night was a sample of how you're treating folks nowadays, then I've had enough. I'd sooner have the blarsted lumbago, any time." He stamped out of the shop, leaving Dolly and John looking after him sheepishly, and 'Enry looking puzzled.

Ben didn't go to the doctors, and neither did his friends. The doctor was still waiting for the patients to turn up, and Dolly was getting more and more worried. The odd villager had called in at the surgery, but the main bulk of the pensioners, who had been such regular callers in Dr. John's time, stayed away, waiting to hear from others what they thought of the newcomer. "I feel sorry for him." said Simon Stead, the retired schoolteacher one morning. "I think I'll go along there myself this morning, and give the others a lead. I'm sure I'm in for a bad cold." I looked at Simon. He had never looked fitter. "I can spare you for an hour," said Maggie, giving me a nudge in the ribs. "Why don't you go along too and get something for that cough of yours?" "Cough?" I said. "Yes. Cough," said Maggie. "Oh, yes," I said. "Cough. I'll go along with you, Simon."

Dr. Hapton held his surgery four mornings each week in the front parlour of one of the villagers cottages, just as Dr. John had done. The lady who lived in the cottage would sit in the corner knitting, and the waiting patients could pass the time by talking to the budgie that hung in its cage in the other corner, or by stroking one of the two black cats that sat in front of the open fire. The parlour-cum-waiting room was built of the same clay lump and wattle as was the rest of the building, and consequently had no sound proofing qualities worth mentioning. It followed that if the patients who were waiting were quiet enough, they were very likely to overhear a good part of the conversation between doctor and patient. The lady of the house did keep a small radio playing quietly in one corner, but if a waiting patient should ever turn it down slightly, she never objected. She was as inquisitive as the rest of us.

Simon and I were sitting together, watching the budgie, when Granny Coster came into the waiting room. She was carrying her little terrier dog under one arm. The lady knitter looked at us with raised eyebrows, but no-one told the old lady that dogs were not allowed in the surgery. We all knew that we would have been wasting our time in doing so, Granny being in the habit of pretending to be insane when being told anything that she didn't want to hear.

When Dr. Hapton called out "Next one please," Granny got to her feet immediately and went into the next room. Simon, who had stood up to take what should have been his turn, shrugged and sat down again. "One person before me won't make all that difference," he said to the lady in the corner. "No," came the reply, "But if there were more than one like Granny Coster in the village, I don't think that the new doctor would want to stay very long." The speaker stood up, and going over to the radio, turned it well down. Neither Simon nor I objected.

Granny greeted the new doctor with a toothless grin. "Mornin," she said, and sat her little dog down in the middle of the doctor's desk. Dr. Hapton looked at the animal with astonishment. "Is there something wrong with it?" he asked. "No," cackled Granny. "There ain't anything ever wrong with 'im. It's me." The doctor made a move towards the dog, intending to place it down on the floor. The dog made no sound, but drew back its lips from its teeth in such a way that the doctor changed his mind, and sat down again instead. "What's wrong with you then?" he asked, watching the dog warily. "It's me poor arm," said Granny. "'Ave a look at it, will yer?" Dr. Hapton reached out and took her outstretched hand in his. The little dog bared his teeth again and looked as if he was prepared to spring at the doctor at any moment. "Does it hurt?" asked the doctor, leaning forward. The dog's teeth closed within an inch of the end of his nose. "Yes," said Granny, in a pathetic tone. "It 'urts something dreadful." The dog looked at Granny adoringly, and then accusingly at the doctor. It inched its way forward on the polished desk top, towards him. "It's only a sprain," said the doctor. The dog leaned menacingly towards him. "It's a pretty bad one though," he said hastily, as much to the dog as to Granny. The animal leaned back again. "If you can wait until I've seen the other patients," said the doctor, to the dog. "Or until Dolly Foster turns up, we'll dress it for you." He didn't like the idea at all of trying to dress the wrist under the critical gaze of the terrier, and was playing for time. "Thank'ee," said Granny, rising to her feet. She tucked the little dog under her good arm, and fumbled in the depths of the pockets of her long black coat. Dr. Hapton sat and gazed mesmerised at the polished top of his desk, and the misted warm patch where the little dog had been sitting. "Here," said Granny. "I only baked this yesterday, you'll enjoy it." Her grubby hand placed an unwrapped currant bun down on the desk, just where the dog had been sitting. "I'll have it later." said the doctor quickly. The little dog struggled under Granny's arm and bared its teeth again as it tried to reach him. "Thank you, thank you," said the doctor, as he changed his mind, and he broke off a piece of the bun and stuffed it in to his mouth. "Delicious," he said, and then in a voice that was unnaturally falsetto, "Next please."

Dolly Foster bumped into Granny as she was coming out of the door. "Oh, it's 'er," Granny cried. "I've got something here for you. She shoved one of the buns into Dolly's hand. Dolly looked at it and blanched. "No thank you, Granny," she said. "I'm on a diet." The little dog under Granny's arm wriggled and bared its teeth at her. "Oh you," said Dolly, wagging a finger at it. "If

you don't shut up, I'll take your temperature for you."
The dog's ears went flat to its head, and it looked at the
ceiling in apparent embarrassment.

Some of the villagers were beginning to accept the
new doctor, but his surgeries seldom had more than a
handful of patients, and he still had a long way to go.
He would be accepted in time, of course, but Maggie
and I still did whatever we could to speed up the process.
Whenever we mentioned the doctor, or illness, when
there were a group of customers in the shop, the conversation always seemed to turn to home cures and her-
bal remedies. This was understandable, as herbs did play
a very large part in some of the concoctions that were
used by the villagers, and onions seemed to play a part
in every one. Maggie and I thought that onions were
Dr. Hapton's rival in the villagers minds, and that if all
the onions in the village were to disappear overnight,
his surgery would be full the next day. We were wrong
though, and it was onions that were largely responsible
for the new doctor being accepted by the rest of the
locals.

Onions could be found in every home in the village.
They hung about in kitchens and sheds, in strings and
bunches, and they were eaten in such huge quantities
that Maggie and I were astounded. The villagers seemed
to regard them as a staple food, along with bread and
potatoes, and apart from eating purposes, they used
onions in those old remedies that had been handed
down by way of example for generation after generation, and still found to be effective in the twentieth century. If a child had earache, then the centre of an onion
would be pared down until it was just the right size to
fit snugly into the ear, then it would be left in the oven
until it was as hot as the child could bear, then it would
be placed in the ear and left there overnight. We were
assured that this treatment worked better than anything

that Dr. Hapton could ever prescribe. I suggested that heat was the main healing agent, and that anything with a texture similar to that of the onion would have the same effect. This was met by a great shaking of heads and gasps of amazement at my ignorance. Didn't I know, I was asked, that the onion absorbed germs, amongst other things? If a hanging pheasant should smell a little too gamey, then an onion placed inside it would absorb all the bad parts of the smell, but leave the good. Likewise, a hot onion, bound over a septic wound, or a boil, would draw out all the poison overnight. Maggie and I were also emphatically assured that an unwanted pregnancy, if caught early enough, could be terminated by the mother-to-be soaking herself in a hot bath filled with boiled onions. When I suggested that this course of action might be an effective way of preventing the pregnancy from occurring in the first place, I was the only one who thought that it was funny. The villagers simply thought that I was ignorant, which of course, I was.

They explained to me at great length that given the undoubted properties of the onion, it followed that the obvious and natural way to keep our systems free from poisons and germs was to eat as many onions as one could, and as often as possible. I said that I doubted the theory, and that a diet of onions might be all very well for a hermit, but the smell of them on a person's breath could be very offensive to others, particularly if the onions were pickled or raw. This remark was greeted by such laughter that I was made to feel quite stupid. The way to avoid the smell, I was told patiently, was to eat a bit of parsley after a meal of onions. Didn't I know that parsley killed the smell? I said that I didn't, but had to admit that in spite of the amounts that were consumed, I had never noticed the smell of onions on anyone's breath.

It was as Maggie and I were cleaning up the Post

Office just after closing time, that we decided to put the parsley theory to the test. Maggie had made a pot of tea and a couple of cheese sandwiches, and we had a bunch of parsley that one of the customers had given to us. Maggie sliced up a couple of raw onions, and stuffed as much into the sandwiches as they would hold. We had each eaten half a sandwich before Maggie spoke. "I think we've done it wrong," she said, with tears streaming down her face. "I think that only one of us should have eaten the onion, then the other could have told whether they smelled or not." "You may be right," I said, gasping for breath, "But if we check our breath now, one of us can eat some parsley, and then we can check again, and see what effect it has had." "Right," said Maggie, opening a box of tissues and taking one. "Let's try it."

"Haa," said Maggie, right in my face. "What was that like?" "I can't tell," I said. "My nose is running." I grabbed one of the tissues, while Maggie wiped her eyes with another. I leant towards her. "Haa," I said. "What do you smell?" "Nothing," she answered. "Atishoo!" "You try again," I said. I closed my eyes, and tried to concentrate on my sense of smell. "Aaah," said Maggie. I smelled nothing. "Aaah." came the sound again. "Don't overdo it," I said. "It's a waste of time." "That wasn't me," said Maggie. "It was you." "No, it wasn't," I said. "It was you. I was standing here with my eyes closed. "Haaa," came the sound again, and Maggie leapt as if she'd been shot. "It must be a ghost," she whispered. "Perhaps the magic onions work on them too." "Haa," came the sound again, and this time it was from the direction of the window. We both turned and stared. There, with its forepaws on the sill, was a large shaggy mongrel. Its teeth were bared in a snarl as it looked at us, two humans with tears running down their faces, apparently snarling at each other. "Ah!" gasped Maggie. "Aaah," answered the dog.

"It's our fault." I said to Maggie. "That poor dog has probably never seen two people acting like this before. He probably thinks that we're preparing for a fight. It's a good thing that he can't talk; just think of it, it would be all round the village by tomorrow, and how on earth could we ever explain to the customers what it was that we were doing?" "I don't know," said Maggie. "But I think you're going to have to, look." She pointed to the

other window, and I looked. Faces filled the square of glass. There were children and pensioners, farmers and housewives, and as they stared at Maggie and me, none of them were smiling. They nudged each other, and slowly dispersed, avoiding our eyes as they went. "Oh dear." said Maggie. "What on earth can they be thinking?" "Only that we're a couple of lunatics." I said. "We can only hope that it doesn't affect our trade. We'll find that out tomorrow."

We did. I opened up the shop and let in the six or seven people who were already waiting there. "Good morning," I called cheerfully, to all of them at once. "Haaaa," they all answered, with one voice.

Dr. Hapton, who had followed the customers into the shop, stood and looked at the villagers in amazement. "I haven't heard a sound like that, from so many throats, since I left the city." he said. He turned to me. "No wonder no-one with a sore throat comes to the surgery, they're all up here, letting you hear their symptoms." He looked round at the locals, and grinned cheerfully. "You'll all be glad to know that your throats sound fine to me." he said. "But I'd like you all to promise me one thing. When your voices get too hoarse, after making all that noise at this poor fellow, you'll call in at the surgery, and let me give you something for your throats. I've got something that acts particularly well in conjunction with onions." The villagers looked frankly at the doctor. They had been weighing him up as he spoke, and there was no hostility in their expressions as they smiled back at him now. Old Charlie seemed to speak for all the others when he answered, and it was obvious that the newcomer had at last broken the ice, and without any help from us. Old Charlie winked at the doctor. "Aaaah," he said.

CHAPTER SEVEN.

SHOW A LEG.

It came as something of a surprise to Maggie and me to discover that the olde worlde features of the Norfolk flint cottages that we city people found so very attractive were not at all appreciated by the majority of the country people who had lived in them all their lives. A good number of the villagers spoke with envy of relatives who lived in modern bungalows, with smoothly plastered walls and ceilings, and no dust-collecting beams. Whistling Jack, the village's jobbing builder, was well aware of this attitude, and the liking of city people for the old fashioned, and throughout his working life, much of the profit that he had made must have come about by this difference in taste between the locals and the newcomers.

Jack never threw anything away. If he modernised a cottage, then the old fittings were removed and stored behind his home, waiting for some restoration job, where they could be used again, and charged for. Jack himself, though he had modernised many a cottage in the village and surrounding area, still lived in a house that was full of exposed beams and crooked walls and doorways.

Matthew Thrower's house was a beautiful example of an eighteenth century Norfolk flint cottage. It had never been altered or spoilt in any way, but it was not at all appreciated by Mrs. Thrower, who complained about the old place so loudly and so long that in the end Matthew agreed to spend quite a large amount of money on the place and have it modernised. Whistling Jack came to the cottage and gave his advice willingly. He got the job. He plasterboarded all the ceilings, covering up the old beams. He flushed all the doors, hiding all the old oak beneath gloss painted plywood. "These old black iron door latches need painting every so often, else they rust," he said to his clients. "I can fit you some nice chrome ones that will never need touching." The Throwers agreed, and allowed Jack to dispose of the old unwanted latches.

Jack fitted a small neat modern fireplace in the recess of the great old red brick one, and covered up the red tiled kitchen floor with the very latest in plastic floor coverings. He treated the outside walls of the cottage with a white cement paint, hiding the beautiful old flints, and then, after the whole interior had been redecorated in the latest colour scheme, Mrs. Thrower declared herself highly satisfied with the result.

It wasn't so very long after this that Matthew was offered a very good job in a different area. A modern house went with the job, and the Throwers didn't hesitate. They put the cottage up for sale. It wasn't on the market for more than a few days before it was bought by a newly married couple fresh from the city. Matthew and his wife commented that they were now glad that they had had all the work done on the cottage, as they had got a far better price than they would have dared to ask if the old cottage hadn't been so well modernised.

The newcomers to the village were a quiet young couple. Doris, a good looking girl, was perhaps a little on the prudish side for one so young, but she soon made friends with the other young wives of the village. Paul, her husband, was a tall and well built fellow, much taken with rugby, and all outdoor sports. The couple soon made themselves known to the vicar, and indicated that they would be regular churchgoers, and would be more than pleased to join in any church activities. "A very welcome addition to our community," the vicar said of them. "It's most heartening to see such enthusiasm amongst people so young."

Jack was pottering about in the yard behind his cottage when the young couple called on him. After introducing themselves they told him that they had moved into the Thrower's' old cottage, and they would want quite a lot of alteration work doing. They would like the old place restoring, so they said, as near as was possible, to its original olde worlde state. Jack looked round at the piles of old red bricks that littered his yard, and at the shed, that was filled to bursting with old black iron fittings from cottage doors and windows, and mentally he licked his lips.

"It just so happens," he said, lying with professional ease, "that I've just had a cancellation on a job that I was due to start on tomorrow. If we can come to an agreement on your job, I can start right away." He quoted his terms, an hourly rate, plus the cost of any materials involved. "That sounds very reasonable to me," said Doris, and wandered off into a corner of the yard to examine an old pump that was lying there. Paul drew Jack to one side, and looked down at the smaller man with an intense expression. "I just want to warn you, before you start," he said, "that I don't want any messing about on this job, not in my house." Jack looked puzzled. "Messing about?" he said. "I'll not be wasting any time, if that's what you're on about. I'll be wanting to get this job over and done with as soon as possible. I've got lots of other work booked, you know. You're just lucky that I can come to your place so soon." "It's not the work that I'm thinking about." said Paul. "It's what *you* are like that concerns me." "Well, I'm noted for being a bit faster than most," said Jack, pursing his lips in one of his whistles as he tried to understand what the customer was getting at. "What do you mean, you're noted for being fast?" said Paul. "I mean that I don't waste time on the job," said Jack, a note of irritation creeping into his voice. "What do you mean?" "I mean, what are you like with women?" said Paul. Jack blinked. "Women?" he said, as though he had never heard of them before. "I'm a very jealous man," said Paul, "and I don't like the idea of my wife having just anybody hanging around the house while I'm away at work. And I'm told that you're a single man." He shrugged his large and muscular shoulders. "Now if you're the type of man who tries to take advantage of a woman while her husband's away, then I'll tell you now, you'd better forget about this job right at the start." Jack whistled, and his mind raced. This job was worth a good deal to him; it should be highly profitable, but if the husband was as unreasonably jealous as this, perhaps it would be wiser for him to have nothing to do with it. He didn't want trouble of that kind. "Look, I've got a good name in this village," he said, drawing himself up as tall as he could, which still left him a good nine inches shorter than Paul. "I've never been noted for messing about in the way that you mean, ask anybody, and I don't like that kind of suggestion. Now, you make up your mind, right now. If you trust me, then we'll forget what you've just said, and I'll get on with the job. If you don't, well, we can both forget that you ever spoke to me." Paul looked at him keenly for a minute. "All right, I believe you," he said. "Start as soon as you like." He turned to go. "But remember," he said, and shrugged his rugger playing shoulders, "any funny business and you'll have me to answer to." "Oh squit," said Jack, "you're off your chump." But he was careful to say it in a voice that was too faint for Paul to hear.

I could have warned Jack, had I known, that Doris and Paul were a little on the narrow-minded side, for I had found this out for myself, when they had visited the shop. I liked them both, but had the feeling that they looked upon me as sort of vice king, and the village shop as a centre of sin. It had started when I kept them waiting for a couple of minutes while I finished a conversation that I was having with a supplier who had phoned me. We had been having difficulty obtaining regular supplies of chicken portions, and was hoping that the new contact would be able to help. The trouble was that more customers wished to buy the leg portions than the wing and breast, and most suppliers naturally wished to supply them in equal quantities. I had decided to try the new man after one young husband had ransacked the deep freeze in temper, brandishing one leg portion as he did so. "Why not take a wing and breast?" I asked him, wincing at the chaos he was causing. "Squit," he answered. "I'll have the other leg; hang it all, he must have had two, mustn't he?"

When Doris and Paul entered, I gave them a smile, and hastily concluded my call. When I had replaced the receiver, I saw that the young couple were eyeing me with a strange hostility. I smiled again, but this time the smile was not returned. Following Doris' and Paul's eyes, I looked at the Post Office blotting pad, which was in front of the phone. As I had phoned, I had been doodling, quite unconsciously. There were only two words on the pad, but they were repeated countless times, in longhand, in heavy block capitals, and sometimes heavily underlined. The two words were, "Legs" and "Breasts".

The next visit that the couple paid us was also the occasion of something of a misunderstanding. I was serving some of the pensioners when an irate housewife stormed in and thumping angrily on the Post Office counter, demanded that we reimbursed her for a pound note that she claimed that she had left in the phone box, and had been stolen. I pointed out that I couldn't be blamed for such a loss, nor could the G.P.O. She banged on the counter again, her anger mounting. "Look, are you responsible for that telephone box?" she demanded. "Well, in a way, yes I am," I admitted. "Well, I left my pound in there, and now it's gone," she said. "Either you're responsible, or you're not. You say you are, so I'll have my money, and make it quick. I'm in a hurry." "Look, I'll report your loss at once," I said. "And I'm very sorry about it, but I can hardly see how you can hold me responsible for it." She rapped on the counter again. "You've just said that you're responsible," she shouted. "You'll have to compensate me." "That's not fair at all," I said feebly.

"Now then, you've got it all wrong, old mawther," said a voice, and Ben shoved his whiskery face up to the Post Office grille, near hers. The housewife flinched. "Now take that daughter o' yourn," said Ben. "You know, that one who works in that big store in the city, bein' rude to folks by way of a livin'. How she got herself pregnant in that there telephone box, last winter, when the lights all failed, that night of the barn dance, but you didn't hold this poor feller responsible for that, did you? It wasn't him as you forced to marry her, anyway." The housewife gasped, and looked for one moment as though she was going to strike the old man, but Ben stood his ground, and gripped his stick tightly as he grinned back at her. With a snort, the irate woman turned and stamped out of the Post Office. Ben winked at me, and then grinned round at Doris and Paul, who had stood listening in horror to the conversation. "She's all right, once you gets to know her," he said. "But she'd do anything to get her hands on an extra penny. There's only one way to deal with people like that." He grinned again, but neither Doris nor her husband returned the grin. They did their bit of shopping with cold politeness and obvious haste, and left as though they were pleased to escape.

Jack was unaware of the young couple's opinion of the village's morals, or their deep suspicion of his own, being a local. He turned up to work on the cottage promptly, and he worked with energy and method. He wanted to finish the work as quickly as possible, and with this in mind, he drove himself, and he surprised Doris, who had always thought that hard work and religion somehow went hand in hand. He didn't stop to rest, and didn't smoke. He didn't stop for a break at all during the morning, even though Doris did keep on offering him cups of tea at regular intervals. "You and your husband are paying me for an hour's work, and an hour's work is what you'll get," he said. At lunchtime he took his sandwiches and headed for his van. "You'll be far more comfortable in the kitchen," Doris called to him, but he shook his head. "I'd better not," he said. "With a husband who's as touchy as the one you've got, it's better if I'm seen to be outside and by myself as much as possible." Doris blushed. "Yes, I see what you mean." she said. "I suppose we both appear to be a little too prim and proper, judging by today's standards, and maybe Paul does go a little too far, but it's better to be like that than to go the other way, isn't it? You hear so much today about the fall in the standard of behaviour." "My standard of behaviour hasn't fallen," said Jack. "It's just the same as it always was." Doris smiled. "I'm sure that it is," she said. "Do you go to church regularly? Paul and I do." Jack gave a small and embarrassed whistle. "No, I don't," he said. "Not very often, in fact hardly ever, unless there's something special on." Doris drew back, as though afraid of becoming contaminated. "I see," she said, her voice definitely colder. "Well, time's flying, and we both have work to do. I think you'd better go and have your sandwiches." She turned away. "In your van," she added.

Jack concentrated on his work. He surprised the couple by his discoveries. Each day, when Paul came home from work, some new feature of his cottage home would be disclosed to him. Old doors of solid oak were discovered, underneath their modern facings. They would, Jack explained, take an awful lot of doing up, but he was sure that he could make them look as though they had never been tampered with. "Expensive, but well worth it," he said. "They are oak after all," Paul told him to go ahead.

Jack discovered that the floor of the kitchen was still covered with the original old red tiles. "Only a few of them missing," he said. "And I think I know where I can lay my hands on some that will match perfectly. Should I buy them for you?" Paul said that he should. "All these window fittings and door catches," said Jack. "They shouldn't be these ugly new ones, not in a place like this. You need the old fashioned black iron ones. They're pretty scarce nowadays, but I know a man who knows a man. Should I buy some on your behalf?" The couple said that he should.

Jack's most exciting discovery was the fireplace. He made a thorough examination of the chimney breast and then told the couple that in his expert opinion there probably was, hidden away behind that potty little modern fireplace, an original olde worlde one, big, and built

110

of old red brick. If they didn't mind the expense of the time involved, and the purchase of a few matching bricks, he could renovate the old fireplace and give the room the character that it lacked. Doris and Paul told him to go ahead, and when the fireplace was revealed, declared that they were delighted.

Jack began to feel a lot happier about the job. Paul now seemed to regard him with far less suspicion, now that he had got to know him, and Doris seemed to be positively friendly at times, though she had never offered him a cup of tea again. His hours had mounted up, and the bill was growing nicely, and he was making a very good profit out of the old materials that he was supplying. In general, he came to the conclusion that his misgivings at the beginning of the job had been unfounded. He saw no reason at all now that the work should not go smoothly until the job was finished and he was paid. He tackled the work with renewed enthusiasm.

The ground floor was completed, and Jack was asked by Paul to renew any worm-eaten floorboards upstairs, and then take a look at the outside of the cottage, and see if the old flintwork could be revealed. "Pleasure," Jack said, and as he worked away upstairs, his mood was so much improved that his whistle returned again, and was heard echoing through the house, though this did nothing to improve his relationship with Doris at all.

It was when Doris was alone in the cottage that the accident happened. Paul had driven off to his work in the city, and Jack hadn't arrived yet. Doris was walking through from one bedroom to the other, her vision obstructed by the pile of blankets that she was carrying, when one of her feet went through a hole in the floor, and she fell. Too late she remembered that Jack had warned her that he had removed one of the floorboards the day before. She wasn't hurt, but she sat there for a moment, getting her breath back, one leg sticking out in front of her, the other one hanging down into the hallway below.

When she had recovered, she tried to get to her feet. She found that she couldn't. The ceiling below, that had opened so obligingly to allow her leg to pass through, now closed like a gin trap every time she tried to withdraw it. Not being the panicking type, Doris sat for a minute, thinking.

She heard a sound in the hallway below. It was Whistling Jack, come to finish off the floorboards. "Er, hello," he called, opening the door and sticking his head through. "Anyone at home? Oh Law!" He gave an exceptionally shrill whistle, even for him, as he spied the shapely leg, dangling before his eyes. "Come and get me out," shouted Doris. "I can't move." Jack was silent for a long minute, as his mind raced. He didn't like this situation one little bit. Paul was not the sort of man who would wait for an explanation if he came home suddenly and found another man messing about with his wife's leg. "Look, I, er, I'd better go off and get some help," he called to Doris. "I ain't never seen a job like this one before, it's sort of right out of my usual line of work. I'd sooner have somebody else here with me, if you know what I mean." "Don't you dare go away," commanded Doris. "And don't you dare tell anyone else. I don't want the whole village to see me like this, or to hear about it either, and what would Paul say?" It was too late. The front door slammed, and Jack was hurrying off down the road.

In a matter of minutes, Doris heard the sound of feet in the hallway below, then there was absolute silence again. "Who is it down there?" she called. "And what are you doing?" There was no reply, only the sound of Old Ben's voice, talking more or less to himself. "I mind the time," he said, dreamily. "When there was a smoked ham a-hanging from the beams in nearly every cottage in this here village. Course, they was the other way up to that, and not nearly as good to look at." "Will you stop talking nonsense and get me out of this!" shouted Doris, her voice getting shriller. There was still no reply, but she heard the sound of a chair scraping on the hall floor below. "Who's that?" she called suspiciously, "What's going on?" "It's only me, missus." said Ben, trying to keep the gloating note out of his voice. "I'm a-looking to see what's to be done." "Don't you dare look at my leg," shouted Doris. "I know all about you dirty old men. You've got nasty minds." There was no reply, and Doris became more and more alarmed, realising the vulnerability of her undignified position. "Get away from my leg," she yelled. "I am away from your leg," said Ben's voice. "Liar!" yelled Doris. "I can feel your breath on it."

"This is a rum job and no mistake, ain't it?" said Jack to Ben. "You know, it might take us some time to get her out of this." He shouted upstairs to Doris. "How does it feel, does it hurt, should I get a doctor?" "No," said Doris, plumping up the blankets as comfortably as she could around her. "I'm all right up here." "The bit that's down here ain't that bad either," said Ben's voice. "Get that horrid old man out of my house," screamed Doris. "And do something to get me out of this." There was the sound of whispering from below, and Doris held her breath and leant her head on one side, trying to hear what was going on. She couldn't make out a word. "Why are you so quiet?" she bawled. "Has that awful old man gone?" "He's gone all right," said Jack. "But I'm hanged if I know what I'm going to do." "Well do something, do anything," commanded Doris. "I'll have to," said Jack. "Ben's only gone to get his camera."

There was a knock on the front door. "Oh goodness, that will be the milkman," called Doris. "You'll have to get rid of him as quickly as you can. Tell him I'll pay him next week, but don't whatever you do let him see me like this." "Fold your leg up as small as you can while I open the door." said Jack. "He might think it's some kind of light fitting or something. His old eyes ain't all that good." Jack opened the door a crack, and told the milkman that the lady was out, and that he'd have to call again. "Right you are," said the man. "By Jove, you've got some work on with that old ceiling Jack. It's in a terrible state, isn't it? I reckon you'll have to go at it with a big hammer and then start again from scratch." Jack closed the door, before the milkman could see any more. "Eeek!" screamed Doris, rage suddenly taking over. "Shush," said Jack. "You'll bring half the village out to see what's going on."

"What are you doing to my leg now?" shouted Doris. "I'm not doing anything to it, I'm thinking." said Jack. "You are, you're touching it, I can feel it." yelled Doris. "You're just as bad as that dirty old man, I knew you were, right from the start." "I can see what it is," said Jack, controlling his temper. "There's a big spider walking up it." "Eeeek." screamed Doris again. "Shall I get it off?" asked Jack, hesitantly. "No, how dare you! Don't you dare lay a finger on my leg," screamed Doris. "And stop staring at it like that." "Well, blarst me, what do you want me to do," bawled Jack, his patience finally at an end. "Oh, I don't know," screamed the prisoner, and she waved her leg about frantically, like a small child in a tantrum. There was a crash, and several pieces of plaster fell to the floor. Suddenly, the leg was free.

Ben arrived panting at the door, an expression of childish glee on his face and his camera in his hand. He was all set to record in close detail the curvaceous captive limb. The young housewife who leapt at him as he entered was not the prim and proper young woman he had come to know. "Oh Gaw," he gasped, as Doris grabbed him by the lapels and thrust him hard up against the wall. Her normally pretty face was twisted into a snarl, and she hissed at him through clenched teeth. "If you ever dare mention a word of this to anyone," she said. "I'll ram that rotten camera right down your scrawny old throat, do you understand?" Ben realised only too well that the female who held him had the strength to carry out the threat. He broke free of her grasp, and brushing down his ragged old jacket in what he hoped was a dignified manner, spoke as casually as he could. "Oh well, I'll be gettin' along then," he said. "I'm glad it all turned out all right in the end, missus." "It could have a very sad ending for you," said Doris. "Just you remember." "Oh I'll remember all right," said Ben, casting a fleeting glance from the ceiling to the young lady's legs. "I ain't never likely to forget it, am I?"

Doris next turned her attention to Jack, who was standing quietly whistling to himself. "And as for you," she said. "If you ever let any of this come out, I'll tell Paul that it was all your fault, and that you did it on purpose, and you know who he's going to believe, don't you?" Jack stopped whistling, and gulped and nodded. "I've forgotten about it already," he said. "Now, I'd better get on with them floorboards. You've paid me for working, not for standing about looking at your, er, mishaps."

After all the time that had been wasted, Jack hurried to complete the work. He replaced the floorboards, and then tackled the outside walls of the cottage, sandblasting the white cement paint off so that the old flintwork stood out proudly once again. Paul and Doris were delighted with the new appearance that it gave to their home. Jack was paid promptly, and he was highly satisfied. He was glad to leave the cottage, where the tension that had built up since the incident of the floorboard had made the atmosphere almost unbearable. Doris never told Paul the full story, but merely let it drop in a casual way that she had almost had a bad fall when her foot had slipped and knocked a hole in the plaster. "It doesn't matter," said Paul. "All that old plaster will have to be renewed eventually anyway." The incident was never referred to by Ben or Jack either, and it seemed that the whole episode had been forgotten. That was until Jack celebrated his escape from the cottage with a few drinks at the village pub. Paul happened to overhear a conversation, and it was then that the trouble really started.

The conversation around the bar was about birth-marks, a baby having been born in the village recently with a rather prominent one on its face. "These here birthmarks are a lot more common than most people think," said Jack knowledgeably to his companion, his vocal chords well lubricated by best bitter. "You don't realise that, 'cos most of 'em are covered up for the biggest part of the time, you see. Now, I'll bet that none of you know this, but Doris, Paul's wife, has a beauty. Like a great big strawberry it is, right here, on her leg." He was pointing to a spot on the thigh of his blue jeans when the bar went quiet, and a deep voice behind him made him freeze. "And just how might you have come to know about that?" the voice asked. Jack turned round slowly and looked up at the speaker, who was a great deal taller than he was. It was Paul. The man that Jack had been talking to backed slowly away from the pair, his eyes wide. Ben, who had been listening with growing apprehension, took his glass of beer and slid it to the other end of the bar. "Oh Gaw, Jack," he said, his whisper loud in the electric silence. "You're all on your own now, bor."

CHAPTER EIGHT.

ROSES ALL THE WAY.

It is a sad fact of human nature that anything that we get for nothing is at best undervalued and at worst unappreciated. Anyone who was unwise enough to organise any function in our local village hall and not charge for admission soon discovered this unpleasant fact for themselves, for those very same villagers who would remain quiet and attentive, determined to get their money's worth, once they had paid, would very soon bring chaos to any free function, regarding it as an unimportant stop-gap in their week's entertainment.

The gang of funsters who were responsible for most of the heckling that went on on these occasions were of mixed ages, but were usually headed by old Ben, and he and his cronies had once been referred to as "The village Mafia," by one demoralised speaker, after they had completely ruined his speech on farm management.

It was no surprise at all to us, therefore, that when a large local firm of rose growers decided to celebrate

117

their half century by staging an "Evening with Roses," with free admission, not only for their employees, but for any other villagers who cared to attend, that things didn't go quite according to plan, even though that plan was an extremely simple one.

The chairman of the company called at the village hall to discuss details of the arrangements with Miss Money, who was, as usual, representing the Village Hall Committee. The evening would commence, he said, with a short talk, given by himself, on the history of the rose, and including some details of the history of his firm. Then there would be dancing, the music being provided by a trio, the musicians being employees of the company. There would be light refreshments, freely available at each interval. "But mainly," said the chairman, "there will be roses. Each lady, as she enters, will be presented with a corsage, and each escort with a rosebud for his buttonhole. But the highlight of the whole evening will be a shower of rose petals," he beamed with pride, "gently falling from the ceiling, at the end of the evening's dancing."

The petals, explained the chairman, were to be strung high up in the ceiling, supported on two long strips of canvas. At the right moment, a string would be pulled, and the canvasses would tip, sending the petals lightly showering down on the dancers, covering them in a fragrant cloud. "A little brainwave of my own," confessed the chairman, modestly. "We tried it out at the annual dance last year, and it was a great success. So effective, so very beautiful." Miss Money, who at times could be very practical, in spite of her fey appearance, immediately suggested a slight increase in the hire charge for the hall, "in view of the extra cleaning that will be necessary because of the petals." The chairman agreed without a quibble. "But there is just one other small point." he said. "I have heard, from previous

118

speakers, about the hecklers of this village. I wouldn't like my speech to be ruined, and I would like you to do something about them, before we conclude our agreement." Miss Money frowned. The hecklers now seemed to be the only fly in the ointment. This was a perennial problem, and one that she had never been able to solve. "There is only one sure way of stopping the hecklers," she said. "And that is to charge for admission. If you do, they'll either stay away, or sit there as quiet as mice, so that they don't miss a word." The chairman shook his head. "No," he said. "This is to be the firm's celebration, and the firm will pay for everything. It will be free." "Then how would it be if we invited Ben, the ringleader, to sit up on the stage, as a sort of guest of honour." said Miss Money slowly. "There will only be yourself, and the vicar, and me of course, to announce you. He might well be flattered by the invitation, and he couldn't very well get up to much mischief there, could he?" The chairman beamed. "Marvellous," he said. "Divide and conquer, what? You should be on my board of directors, my dear, with a mind like yours." Miss Money blushed. "Well, I think that covers everything," she said. "Yes," said the chairman, holding out his hand. "And I'm sure that everyone will have a very good time. With your help, I'm going to give this village an evening that it will remember, and hang the expense." "That's good to hear." said Miss Money, retrieving her dainty hand from his, "And of course, if they do remember it, it will be a very good advertisement for your firm, won't it?" The chairman winced, as though she had slapped him. "My dear lady." he said. "That thought had never even crossed my mind."

The evening came, and the village hall was buzzing with activity. Men from the rose growing firm had been working all day long, and the hall was bedecked with roses. Even the village hall cat, drowsing on a radiator beneath the window was wearing a rosebud, tied with a ribbon around its neck. When the guests began to arrive, they found that the entrance had been disguised as a rose covered archway, and the ladies gasped with pleasure as they entered. The only complaint that was heard came from old Ben, as soon as he came in. "Oh Gaw," he gasped. "What's all that ruddy smell then?" Miss Money looked at him with ill-disguised disapproval. "That is not a smell," she said. "That is the scent of roses." Ben thrust his whiskery chin out and wrinkled his nose. "Well, it smells like a smell," he said. "You mind that it don't get into them sandwiches." He turned away, intent on finding himself a seat in the hall, where his cronies were already congregating. "Oh, Ben," called Miss Money, smiling sweetly, in spite of her nervous tension. "You've been invited to sit up on the stage, with the speaker, to sort of, well, represent the villagers." She paused, holding her breath, uncertain how the old man would react. Ben beamed at her, his stubble parting and his gappy teeth showing. "Gaw, that's nice!" he said. "Does that mean that I gets the same refreshments as they do then?" "Er, yes, of course," said Miss Money, her white gloved fingers crossed behind her back. Ben spat on his hands, and then wiped them over his whiskers and his hair, then he straightened his ragged old jacket, and rubbed the toe of each boot on the back of his trouser leg. "Right! I'm ready, lead on," he said, and he followed Miss Money towards the stage. The chairman caught Miss Money's eye as she passed, and he raised his eyebrows in a silent question, and nodded towards Ben. Miss Money looked back at him gravely from under her large flowery hat, but then raised one white gloved thumb, and winked.

Ben sat up on the stage and surveyed the crowd. He waved and grinned to a few of his friends, and then, as he could think of nothing better to do, settled himself as comfortably as he could in his chair, and waited for the proceedings to commence. Miss Money went to the front of the stage, and called for silence. She bade everyone welcome, and after introducing the chairman with commendable brevity, left the stage. The chairman got to his feet, and after a long and fascinated look at Ben, took some papers from his pocket and started off on a speech that was far too long to hold the attention of the crowd for long. The audience soon found something else to divert them though. Len, the village poacher, had made his entrance, and unknown to him, his large Labrador dog had sneaked in after him, and was creeping about in the forest of legs, searching for its master. The dog squeezed itself in between the first row of chairs and the second, and then pushed itself quietly but persistently along, sniffing methodically at each ankle as it went. There wasn't quite enough room for both dog and legs, so the members of the audience each pushed their chairs back slightly as the dog pushed through. This had a strange rippling effect that was quite unnerving when seen by the chairman from the stage. He couldn't, from his position, see the dog. "A symbol of all that is England," he was saying, and the third row rippled away from him slowly. He cleared his throat nervously. "Then, in the Wars of the Roses," he said, and the fourth row beat a slight but definite retreat from him. He fingered his collar, and with an effort, went on. "Each side choosing the rose as its emblem," he said, and twitched as he saw that the fifth row were now on the move. His eyes flickered sideways, towards the wings, but Miss Money, whom he was looking for, was nowhere to be seen. He couldn't for the life of him understand why the audience should back away from him in this manner, but hoped that it wasn't meant to be a criticism of his speech. He increased his speed, realising that as things were going, before he had finished, the whole audience might very well disappear backwards through the door, if they kept up their present rate of movement. A moment later he began to wonder whether his change of speed had been wise. As he spoke, the crowd were still moving, still rippling away as though under the command of some invisible general. But they were no longer in retreat. Now the movement was towards him.

The dog, having forced the back row up against the wall, and still not found its master, had started to retrace its steps. There was nowhere else for the chairs to go now, except forwards. The speaker paused and tried to assess the mood of the audience. Were they angry? Had he said something terrible, without knowing it, and broken some frightful local taboo? He swallowed, and went on. The crowd kept advancing. He decided to cut his speech short. He had heard that people in crowds could get carried away, out of control of themselves, and do things that singly and separately they would never do. He gabbled through his last few sentences, perspiration breaking out on his forehead. What would happen if he didn't finish in time? What would they do when they all ended up crushed in a heap at the foot of the stage, would they then attack him?

Ben found the whole proceedings a good deal more boring than he had imagined. He was placed rather closer to the wings than he would have wished, and he could only see half of the audience. He was seated next to the vicar, and there seemed to be little opportunity for amusement in that direction. He settled himself even further down in his seat. He pulled his hat well forward to cut out the glare, and closed his eyes. He was away in that dreamy state between sleeping and waking when he was jerked upright by a violent nudge from the vicar. "Look," the reverend whispered, and pointed towards the wings. Ben looked. From the side of the stage they were being examined by the small beady eyes of a field mouse. The little creature seemed to sense that it was in some danger, for it suddenly panicked, and running to Ben's feet, tried to hide itself in the ragged bottoms of his trouser legs. The speaker's hat was on his chair, and without a second's hesitation Ben reached across the vicar, grabbed the hat, and placed it over the mouse. Then he placed his feet on the brim, and turning to the vicar, winked. "Oh, well done." said the vicar, relieved that he had a countryman on the stage with him.

The chairman brought his speech to a close, his nerves getting the better of him as the crowd kept on creeping. He collapsed into his chair and thought longingly of the bottle of whisky that was sitting on the refreshment table. Miss Money bobbed up again, right on cue, and after thanking the chairman, but failing to wring a round of applause out of the audience, said that if the men of the audience would take the chairs to the back of the hall and stack them there, the dancing could commence. Ben, in the meantime, had resumed his former position, with his eyes closed. As he relaxed, so did his foot's pressure on the brim of the hat. The hat took its opportunity, and made its bid for freedom. It began very slowly edging its way along the stage, in full view of the audience. Miss Money, interrupted in her speech by the sniggering from the crowd, looked round, and saw the mobile hat. She knew immediately what was going on. This was another of those silly tricks that she had come to expect from certain of the villagers. She regretted now that she had ever suggested inviting Ben onto the stage and thus presenting him with the opportunity to sabotage the proceedings at close quarters. At the other side of the stage there would be, she was sure, one of the local hecklers, pulling on a thin thread of some sort, and giving the impression that the hat itself was trying to move. She pursed her lips with annoyance, and bending, made grabbing movements in front of the quivering hat. Her groping fingers contacted nothing, and the audience, under the impression that they were witnessing a conjuring trick, cheered and clapped. Miss Money grabbed the hat and lifted it. The mouse crouched trembling on the stage. Miss Money, startled, gave a little scream. The village hall cat, which had been drowsing on its window sill, and hadn't seen the mouse before, suddenly came to its senses, and sprang. Len's Labrador, which hadn't seen the cat before, stopped sniffing at ankles, and growled and charged. Len, who hadn't realised until then that his dog was in the hall, shouted, and ran. The chairman, realising that the hat that Miss Money was waving about was his, made a grab for it, but missed, and fell off the stage.

Ben stood up, suddenly wide awake, and sensing that he was missing some fun. The lady who was in charge of the refreshments, who had taken an instant dislike to the ragged old man as soon as she had set eyes on him, and had seen him doing something suspicious with the chairman's hat earlier, came out of the wings like an avenging angel, and clunked him around the ears, sending him back into his seat again.

Ten minutes later, the chairs had been stacked, the animals removed, and dancing was in full swing. Miss Money had discarded her hat and gloves, and was being whisked gracefully around the floor by the vicar. The trio were performing very well indeed, and the villagers were enjoying themselves. The earlier upset appeared to have been forgotten by everyone except the chairman, who concealed himself in a corner behind a table that was piled high with refreshments, and poured himself a generous whisky from his bottle. Ben left the stage, and joined his friends at the edge of the dance floor, but kept his weather eye open for the free refreshments. More people arrived, and the latecomers joined in the

dancing with gusto. The evening at last promised to be indeed one that the village would remember.

Maggie and I arrived later than most others. The paper work that went with the Post Office had kept me busy long after tea time. I was thankful for the opportunity to sit quietly at the edge of the dance floor and enjoy the pleasant scene, and the conversation. Maggie was claimed by the vicar, and whisked away round the floor. Miss Money seemed to be content to converse, but showed no sign of wanting to dance. Whether this was due to her energetic exertions with the vicar, or her previous experience with my two left feet, I didn't know.

"I think it's about time to call for an interval." said Miss Money to the chairman. He nodded, and took another drink. Ben appeared from nowhere, grinning expectantly. Miss Money went over to the trio, and gave them a pre-arranged signal. At the end of the next four bars the musicians stopped playing, and the dancers left the floor and flocked towards the refreshments.

"I've decided that it would be a very good idea if I brought the proceedings to a close a little earlier than I had previously planned," said the chairman unsteadily to Miss Money. "Er, while everyone is happy, and before anything else goes wrong," he added weakly. "I don't think I could stand any more." Miss Money looked at him closely, and then at the half full whisky glass on the table, "No, you don't look to me as if you could stand a great deal more," she said. "I've got a cold coming on, I think." said the chairman, avoiding her eyes. Miss Money looked around at the groups of happy and relaxed guests. "They're all enjoying themselves so much," she said. "The evening is turning out to be a great success." "Hmm," said the chairman, looking past her to Ben, whose stubbly face was covered in crumbs as he steadily chomped his way through a huge pile of sandwiches. "I'll compromise," he said. "We'll give it another three quarters of an hour, that is if nothing goes wrong, and then we'll let the petals down." Miss Money didn't approve, but like the lady she was, she nodded her head in acquiescence. "You might have quite a bit of food left over, unless you can fit in another couple of intervals." she said. The chairman watched with disgust as Ben and his friends reloaded their plates. "I don't think so," he said.

No incident occurred to mar the last minutes of the dance, and only when the chairman saw that Ben and company had helped themselves to the last of the free food did he grip his notes that he had brought for the closing address and mount the stage. Now was the time for him to call a halt, before the hecklers became bored. He gave the signal for his foreman to let the shower of petals down on the dancers.

The foreman, who had been waiting patiently at his post all evening, lest some prankster should cause the petals to fall too soon, was an elderly man, slim and wiry. He was highly skilled at his profession of rose growing, though not equally adept at showering rose petals down from village hall ceilings. He grasped the cord that ran from the canvasses down the wall, and tugged. Nothing happened. He tugged again, harder, giving his employer a reassuring smile over his shoulder as he did so. Again, nothing happened. He heaved, the veins in his neck bulging. Nothing again. He scrabbled at the cord frantically, leaping into the air and bracing both feet against the wall. Not a petal fell, but most of the crowd stopped dancing and gathered round to watch him. He attacked the cord in a frenzy, leaping two feet up it and muttering rude descriptions of the petals that could be heard quite distinctly over the sound of music. The trio stopped playing, as hardly anyone was now dancing, and the foreman, suddenly realising that he was now the focus of attention, and making a spectacle of himself, relaxed in despair, fatigue replacing his nervous energy. He slumped down in the angle of the wall, a small damp heap of wrinkled blue serge.

Miss Money came to the rescue of the chairman, who was standing woodenly on the stage. With her air of authority restored, now that she was wearing her gloves and wide brimmed hat again, she joined the chairman, and announced that there would be another ten minute interval. When the dancers had dispersed she turned to the unhappy chairman. "You must make those petals fall," she said. "The dancers won't go home until you do. They've been looking forward to it so much, since you advertised it so well." The chairman looked over to his foreman, who had been revived by this time. The man looked at the ceiling and shook his head. The chairman groaned, and took another sip of the glass of whisky that he had brought with him and stood at the side of the stage. At that moment Whistling Jack appeared out of the crowd.

"Er, I couldn't help noticing that you were having a bit of trouble," said Jack, looking up at the canvasses and whistling thoughtfully. "I thought I might be able to help, being, well a sort of practical man." "Tell us quickly, if you have an idea," said Miss Money, snapping her fingers with an impatience that was right out of character. The chairman only looked at the slight blue-denimed figure and groaned again. "Well you'll never get both lots down, not without an awful lot of trouble," said Jack, looking at the canvasses. "But if you can unlock the cupboard in the back room, and get your hands on that vacuum cleaner that's in there, I'll stick it up top, pointing backwards, so that it'll blow one lot of petals down. They're pretty powerful, them cylinder models, it should blow a few old petals about with no bother." "Well, half a loaf would be better than no bread, at this point." said Miss Money, and even the chairman perked up a little, and looked at Jack with some respect. "Good man," he said. "If you can do that, I can give my little speech, and then get off home and forget that I've ever been here."

The dancers were back on the floor, and the trio playing again. Jack, with the vacuum cleaner now installed overhead, took up a position near the electricity switch. The foreman watched him from a safe distance, shaking his head pessimistically. Jack looked towards the stage, and gave a cheery thumbs up signal to the harassed chairman, who took another gulp from his glass, and then ran a hand over his hair, straightened his tie, and stepping forward, raised his hand. The trio stopped playing, the dancers looked towards the stage expectantly. "My dear friends." said the chairman, avoiding any direct glances from any of his alleged friends. "I must apologise for the delay, but at last the moment has arrived. What better way could there be of ending an "Evening of roses" than,—." He nodded to the waiting Jack, who immediately switched on.

The comparative silence of the hall was at once filled with what could very easily have been the sound of an ocean going liner lost in a deep fog. The chairman's lips could be seen to be moving, but not a single word could be heard. The refreshments lady, busy with her cleaning up and unaware of the vacuum cleaner, clapped her hands over her ears and screamed hysterically. Len's dog appeared briefly in the doorway, and showing the whites of its eyes, bit the nearest dancer, and left. The petals did come down, but not in the gentle shower that had been promised. They descended heavily in one large damp lump that landed on a slightly built matron and drove her to her knees. The noise continued, and the petals were followed by a rain of dust and grit from the ceiling that covered the crowd in seconds. The chairman gave up, and fleeing the stage, locked himself in the gents. The dancers, some of them muttering threats about a lynching, left the floor and went to collect their coats. Miss Money went to the chairman's whisky glass, and drained it at a gulp.

The dancers had gone, hecklers and all, and the chairman was also ready to leave. He stood and surveyed the deserted village hall in much the same way as Napoleon might have surveyed Moscow. "I thought that if I took the filter bag out of the cleaner it would give it a bit more power," explained Jack, shuffling his feet. "Never mind that now," grated the chairman. "Forget it. Thank heaven you didn't have two vacuum cleaners in the place, that's all. Those other petals are better left where they are." As if in answer to his remark, there came a loud twanging, and the remaining petals fluttered down into the now deserted dancefloor in a graceful cloud. "Oh." cried Miss Money. "Aren't they just too beautiful?" The chairman's lips quivered, and he held on to his self control only with a superhuman effort. "Beautiful," he said bitterly. "A beautiful end to what I can assure you has been the very worst evening that I have ever spent in my whole life. Thank heaven that it's over, and thank heaven that there's nothing else left that can possibly go wrong." As he finished speaking there was another twang, and the second canvas tipped. There were no petals to fall this time, only the vacuum cleaner, which fell with a frightening crash, breaking into several separate sections as it landed on a chair, and rolling in bits over the dance floor. The chairman gave a high pitched laugh as he looked at the debris. "At least that is your loss, and not mine," he said. "It's just about the only thing that has happened tonight that doesn't affect me." "I'm afraid that it does," said Miss Money, hesitantly. "I'm afraid that it's landed on your hat."

CHAPTER NINE.

A LOAD OF FUN.

Saturday night in the village pub was always a busy time, and the conversation of the regulars, often both entertaining and instructive, was a great attraction, particularly to strangers, and newcomers such as myself. A great deal of knowledge on a variety of subjects could be gained by sitting quietly in a corner and just listening. It was by doing just this that I first heard about club root, and swedes.

Swedes were a popular crop in the village, and this particular year, although they had apparently grown well enough, once they had been lifted they had all been found to be suffering very badly indeed from club root disease. This applied to all the gardens in the district, whether large or small, and whatever their position.

"Burn 'em," said Percy, the village's most expert gardener. "Don't make a compost of 'em, whatever you do, burn 'em, then lime the land well, and leave off growin' 'em for a year, then you should be all right." "You can feed 'em to livestock though, can't you?" said another gardener optimistically. "My old goat will eat 'em all right, in fact she eats 'em out of the garden whenever she gets the chance." "You can feed 'em to your old goat if you like," said Percy. "But if you do you'll have club root forever more. What goes in one end comes out the other. Burn 'em."

"Talking of burning," said Ben, sliding up beside Old Charlie and speaking out of the side of his mouth, with exaggerated caution, "Have you seen what's on the bonfire?" Charlie started. He had been miles away, deep in his own thoughts, and the sight of his friend's distorted features came as something of a shock. "What are you talking like that for?" he asked. "What's gone wrong with your mouth? Won't it open any more than that? It's probably a stroke that you've had, and didn't know. You'll have a job getting that beer down by the looks of it." Ben frowned. "Be quiet can't you," he said. "I'm trying to tell you something without the whole pub hearing me. Have you seen what's on the bonfire?" "Course I haven't," said Charlie. "At least not close up. I can see the pile well enough from here though, and it looks like the usual sort of stuff to me." The village held its communal bonfire in a field only a short distance from the village pub, and though it was visited regularly enough by the children during its construction, few of the older men had reason to go near enough to the site to see what was actually on the heap.

"There's bags o' logs on it," whispered Ben to Charlie, turning up his collar and pulling his hat well down over his eyes. "Great big paper potato sacks they are, full o' good logs." He looked over his shoulder to make sure that no-one was overhearing his conversation. "They'd come in very handy you know, what with winter coming on." "Well, winter ain't here yet," said Charlie. "So there's no need for you to go wrapping yourself up like

132

that. George will put a couple of his logs on the fire if your cold." "I'm not cold," said Ben impatiently. "I just don't want to have folks recognising me, that's all." "Why not?" said Charlie. "Anyway, if you wanted to disguise yourself, the only way to do it would be to grow a foot taller." Ben gritted his teeth. "You must be getting old." he hissed. "I mean it's a pity we can't get our hands on some o' them logs, before they all go up in smoke on bonfire night." Charlie looked shocked. "You can't go around pinching from the kids' bonfire," he said. "It wouldn't do." "Not pinchin'," said Ben, as though the very thought pained him. "Just sort of swappin', that's all. Why, I put an old mattress on there meself, only this morning. That's when I saw the logs." "I'll bet an old mattress of yours won't burn like logs," said Charlie. Ben ignored the remark, and went on. "As long as we make sure that they've got something to burn, I don't see as it matters." Charlie shrugged. "What's the difference, we could never move 'em anyway," he said. "So it's no use talking." "Why not?" said Ben. "We could easily cart 'em away if we had something to pull 'em in." Charlie shook his head. "I'm not as good at that sort o' thing as I used to be," he said. "It sounds like a lot of hard work to me." "Not if we get Percy in on it," said Ben, playing the ace that he had been hiding up his sleeve. "He's got an old car and a trailer, don't forget." At last a slight gleam of interest came into Charlie's eye. "You might have something there, after all," he said. "You go and have a word with Percy, and see what he thinks. And you can get me another beer while you're up on your feet."

Percy was all in favour of the idea, but didn't like the thought of using his car. "We'll have to go early in the morning, before folks are about," he said. "And the old bus ain't so good at starting, not when it's cold. It makes a bit of noise anyway, and we don't want to go waking folks up. And what if we got it stuck in the field, it would look bad, wouldn't it?" "Never mind," said Ben, determined to get his hands on the bags of logs. "We'll just take the trailer. Surely the three of us can drag it along, can't we?" Percy nodded. "It ain't all that far," he said. "And two of us have pulled that trailer many a time, when it's been full of farmyard muck." Charlie still had his doubts, but carried along on the wave of enthusiasm generated by the other two, nodded his agreement. The three arranged to meet at Percy's home the next morning, well before dawn; then, drinking up their beer, they left, Percy and Charlie going out together, Ben following, collar turned up, and pressed against the wall.

The owls were still screeching, and the village street as quiet as the churchyard when the three pensioners set out on their expedition. They walked the lane in stealthy silence, trundling the trailer along the middle of the road and speaking in whispers. The route to the bonfire site was crossed by the railway line, and the road was barred by a couple of manually operated gates. Anyone on foot would use a small gate to one side, and trust to his senses to tell him if a train was coming. With the trailer, the three had to observe the rules that were laid down for all wheeled vehicles. The procedure was clearly set out on a notice board. They had to lift a telephone, which was housed in a small hutch on a post, press a button, and when the signalman up the line answered, ask if it was clear to open the gates and cross. "You do it," said Ben to Percy. "And disguise your voice. You know how some of these people talk." Percy picked up the phone and pressed the button. With his free hand he held his nose, and pursing up his lips in a hideous fashion, said in a high squeaky voice, "Is de line all clear to crosh pleash." "Oh, hello, Percy," came the signalman's voice. "What the devil are you doing about at this hour? Yes, the line's clear, you can cross." Percy slammed down the receiver. "Blarsted busybody," he grunted, and swung the gate open.

They crossed the line and closed the gate, and trundled on down the still drowsing country lane. The occasional owl screeched as they went, and a distant cockerel, impatient for the dawn, crowed now and then half heartedly. Apart from that, their journey was uneventful. They saw no other human being, and as far as they knew, no other human being saw them.

It was Old Charlie who first began to flag. It had been some time since he had walked any distance, and his legs began to tire. At Ben's suggestion he climbed into the trailer. "You save your strength for coming back." he said, anxious to keep morale high.

Charlie perched up on the front of the vehicle, like a grotesque figurehead on some small ship, the faint light gleaming on his bald head and spectacles. Ben chuckled at the sight. "If them kids could see you now, they'd stick you up on top of that bonfire," he said. "I wouldn't mind that," said Charlie, "Providing they stuck you down at the bottom with all the other rubbish." Ben opened his mouth to answer, then changed his mind. He had to nurse Old Charlie along, not upset him.

Charlie seemed to be quite unconcerned by the fact that because the trailer had only two wheels, he was completely in the hands of the other two ancients. If they had lost their grip, or allowed the balance of the trailer to shift, Charlie would have been suddenly tipped out onto the road. They didn't lose their grip, or their balance. They strolled along, pushing the towbar between them, as if the trailer was some outsize perambulator, with an enormous bald baby aboard. Charlie actually enjoyed the ride.

They came to the bonfire field, and easily located the sacks. They were just as Ben had described them, and even Charlie managed a slight grin at the sight. There were twenty sacks all told, more than they could reasonably carry in the trailer. When they had loaded as many as they could, they stood back and looked at the remainder. "It's a darn shame to leave 'em," said Ben ruefully. "They'd see us right through Christmas." "We've got fifteen bags on though," said Charlie. "That's five apiece. It ain't bad." "Still," said Ben. "If we'd brought a bit o' rope with us, we could have got another bag each on top." He went to the towbar and lifted it. "We'd still be able to move 'em all right," he said. "This trailer ain't heavy." "Well we ain't got a bit o' rope," said Charlie impatiently. "So let's take what we've got and forget the rest." "Whistling Jack," said Percy. "He's always got plenty of rope lying about his place, and he only lives a step down the road." "He won't be up at this hour," said Charlie. "And you can't go and wake him." "We don't have to," said Ben. "We can borrow a bit of old rope and have it back again before he gets up. He'll never even know we've had it." "You're right, let's go," said Percy, and set off. Ben went with him, at an eager pace, but Old Charlie followed with some reluctance.

Jack was awakened by the sound of his van door being opened with a creak. He got out of bed, and going to the window, looked out. He saw three figures moving furtively around his old vehicle. "Blarst me, I've got burglars," he said to himself. "And there's a whole gang of them, far too many for me to tackle." Hastily pulling on his clothes he crept down the stairs and let himself quietly out of the back door. He stood trembling in the shadows as he watched the criminals at work, and when they moved away, Jack followed, keeping well out of sight. As the furtive three made their way back to the bonfire site, Jack became more and more curious. The bonfire pile was in the middle of the field, and there was no cover, so Jack had to be content with peering round a tree at the edge of the field and watching the three from a distance. He couldn't hear what was being said, but he could see the trailer, and its load of sacks. He scratched his chin and whistled silently. "That's the funniest getaway vehicle I've ever seen," he told himself.

The extra sacks were loaded aboard by the three elders.They placed them so that most of the weight fell on the back of the trailer, so as to keep the towbar high off the ground. The rope was secured firmly over the load, and the now overtaxed vehicle creaked its way along the lane, back towards the level crossing.

Charlie, who had been complaining about feeling tired again, had the lighter task of steering. He did this by walking along in front and holding the towbar. The other two were at the back, pushing. The lane was level for most of the way, and once the trailer was moving, it took very little effort to keep it rolling along. The extra few sacks on top though, had made the balance of the cart precarious to say the least.

Jack was having some difficulty in following the gang without being seen. He managed to keep behind the hedges and out of sight when the lane was wandering between the fields, but when it passed through a small copse, he found himself making a lot more noise than he would have wished. Twigs snapped under his feet and brambles clawed at his clothes. After he had stumbled several times, he paused, thinking it better to allow the trailer to get well ahead, so that he could leave the trees, and follow along the verge. He was standing quietly, when a voice spoke, just behind him. "Stand quite still, this is the police." it said. Jack stood. "Where's the gun?" the voice said. Jack shook. "Gun?" he said. "What gun?" "Come on," said the voice. "All you poachers have a gun hidden away somewhere, where's yours?" "I've no gun," said Jack. "And I'm no poacher." "Then what are you doing in these woods, and at this hour?" said the voice. "I'm on the track of a gang of thieves." said Jack,

"And you should be helping me to catch them, instead of keeping me here while they escape." The voice laughed heartily. "You won't need any help in catching them, Jack." it said. Jack turned round. "I know your voice," he said. "You're not the police." "No, I'm not," said Len the poacher, "But I could have been, couldn't I?" "You've got a nerve," said Jack. "I hope that P.C. Danby catches up with you one of these nights." Len laughed again. "Oh, I wouldn't have played that trick on you if I hadn't known just where Danby was at this very minute. I reckon those old boys know his where-abouts as well, that's why they chose this morning for their little outing." "What is it, Len?" said Jack. "What are they stealing?" "Well it's not stealing, really." said Len. "It's more like poaching, I suppose, and you wouldn't expect me to tell you about that, would you?"

"Steady now," said Charlie softly over his shoulder. "There's a bit of a slope coming up." "What did you say?" asked Percy, from the rear. "I said slow," said Charlie, grunting as the trailer nudged him gently from behind. "Here, that means we can let up for a bit," said Ben, wiping his brow as he stopped pushing. "It's funny, but I didn't notice this slope when we were coming." Percy also straightened up, and ran a finger round the inside of his collar. "These here logs give out a bit of heat," he said. "Yes, they're as hot as coal, if you cart 'em about long enough," said Ben. "Hey, what was that?" A grinding noise came from the front of the trailer, and a shower of sparks spurted from the road surface. The trailer had begun to leave them behind. With its heavy load helping it along, it was receding down the lane at a steadily increasing pace. The two started running, after it.

At the front, Charlie, with both feet off the ground, was clinging to the trailer for dear life. The towbar, which he had let go when the speed had got too much for his old legs, was scraping along the road, bringing sparks from the surface. Charlie forgot his quiet whispering tones, and shouted to the other two at the top of his voice. "Stop the thing," he yelled. He thought of jumping, but the trailer was now going far too fast for him to risk leaping onto the spark infested road. His eyes, peering through his crooked spectacles, saw terrible danger looming ahead, and his voice grew louder. "Stop it," he roared. "I can see the gates a-comin, and they're closed."

Ben and Percy followed the trailer, moving as quickly as they could. Behind them came Jack, dodging round the hedges, and watching the procession with mystified eyes. Where the lane passed an entry to a field, the road surface was badly rutted. The towbar, travelling along in front of the trailer at a fair speed now, hit the ruts, and stopped. The trailer gave one gigantic heave, as if trying to pole vault itself upside down, and then it stopped. At the front of the strange vehicle, Charlie's grip was wrenched away, and he was catapulted along the verge. He disappeared with astonishing speed through a gap in the hedge.

Ben and Percy arrived, panting. Bending down, they peered at their partner through the hole in the hedge. "Are you all right?" asked Ben, wondering to himself even as he spoke, whether two men alone could manage the trailer. "Oh, yes, I'm just fine," said Charlie, picking up his glasses, which had landed in a cow pat, and wiping them on the dew-damp grass. "I'm having a wonderful time. I'd sooner be doing this any old time than lying at home in my bed." Behind them, Jack took the opportunity to leave cover, examine the trailer and its load briefly, then shoot back behind the hedge again.

The three old timers adjusted the load of sacks, and then set off towards the crossing gates. This time Ben picked up the phone. He gave the other two a knowing wink, and then said, in a voice that indicated extreme insanity, "Cad I go ober at de bobent?" "Oh, hello Ben," came the signalman's voice. "Yes, you can cross, but there's a train due in ten minutes, so don't you and Percy hang about, will you." Ben banged the instrument down. "It's a blarsted wonder he didn't ask how Old Charlie was." he said.

They pushed the gates open, and had pushed the trailer about halfway across the lines when it stopped. "Come on together," said Ben. "It ain't heavy." They heaved in unison, but the trailer didn't move. "Look," said Percy, going down on his hands and knees. "I see what's wrong. The sleepers here are all sort of worn and crooked. They're not smooth like the road is. We're never going to get it across, not with the little wheels that it's got and the load that its carrying." "Well let's pull it back again, till the train's gone." said Ben, and they strained in the opposite direction. The trailer stayed put. "What are you going to do now?" said Charlie, a note of resignation in his voice. "You mean what are we going to do," said Ben. "You don't seem to be helping very much. Don't forget that if the train hits this lot, that's the end of your logs as well as ours." "Oh I don't know," said Charlie. "I reckon there'd still be enough bits lying about for me to pick up a bag or two tomorrow." "They wouldn't let you." said Percy. "They'd keep all the logs for evidence." "I wasn't thinking about the logs," said Charlie. "I was thinking about this blarsted trailer."

"There's only one thing we can do now," said Ben. "We've got to carry the bags across, one by one, and then we can manage the empty trailer. We ain't got no option. That train's a-comin'." Groaning, the other two agreed. They set to work, they untied the rope and grabbed the sacks, moving as quickly as they possibly could. They passed and repassed each other at a bow-

legged run, grumbling and swearing as they went. "Whose clever idea was it to take so many bags?" complained Charlie. "Cheer up, you'll be glad of them in a few weeks' time," said Ben, trying to hide the fact that he was on the point of collapse. A few yards away, Jack watched them over the hedge, shaking his head, and whistling soundlessly to himself.

They removed the bags, and then dragged the empty trailer across the lines, and closed the gates in the nick of time. The train thundered by, casting its flickering light over the three figures panting by the gate. After a minute or two, Ben spoke. "I reckon we're home and dry now." he said, anxious to keep up his companions' spirits for the final stage of the operation. "Oh no, you ain't," said a voice, and the three jumped, Old Charlie's breath leaving his lungs with an audible whistle. Whistling Jack appeared through a gap in the hedge. "Now what the devil do you think you're about?" he demanded. "You're all far too old to take up burgling, and anyway, why pick on me?" "We only borrowed a bit of old rope." said Ben. "We had a few things to move, and needed one." "Yes, a few sort of poached things to move," said Jack. "That ain't none of your business," said Ben. "My rope's my business and it's not an old one." said Jack. "You're lucky I didn't call the police and have you arrested." "Danby's away," said Percy. "Well I could have got the gun out and shot you," said Jack. "I wouldn't have been blamed for it." "Look, we only borrowed your rope, we didn't pinch it," said Percy. "We just didn't want to wake you. We would have put it back before breakfast time, there was no need to come a-spyin' on us." "Well," said Jack, his manner softening slightly, "I suppose that if I get the rope back all right, there's no harm done. But I do need it for a job I've got on today; I bought it special, it's a new one, and I can tell you it cost a lot of money." He looked at the three pensioners and shook his head. "I'll leave you to your fun and games, but remember, I must have that rope back in time to start work." He turned and walked away down the lane. Before he had gone more than a few yards, his good nature took over, and he began to whistle again.

The dawn was well on its way. The lane that had been so quiet on their first journey was now loud with birdsong. The three men, resting by the roadside, began to feel better. Their task was almost over, they had almost accomplished their mission. It had been a harder journey than they had planned, but they had managed it, and now it was a beautiful day. A blackbird sang in the hedge, and a couple of rabbits came out and played on the verge. Ben grinned at his companions. "Makes you feel good, don't it?" he said. "It ain't a bad old world, all considered." He got to his feet, filled with a new energy. "We'll soon get this little lot home." he said, "Then while you take the rope back to Jack's place, I'll get you a bit of breakfast. I've got a bit of home cured bacon, off one of 'Enrys pigs. It'll go down a treat after this little caper." His two friends perked up at the thought, but Charlie didn't actually smile. "I'll get the rope," said Percy, and he got to his feet and went back towards the crossing gate.

"Oh, Gaw!" came Percy's voice, and the other two, alarmed by his tone, went quickly over to him. He was standing in the middle of the crossing, staring at the ground with an expression of utter dismay. They followed his gaze, and once more Old Charlie's breath whistled through his teeth. They had flung the rope down when they had so hurriedly unloaded the trailer, and it had fallen in loose circles. It had fallen across the line though, and the train had passed since then. Jack's new and expensive rope was now lying neatly chopped into a series of three foot lengths. "Oh Gaw, oh Law!" said Ben, his high spirits suddenly gone. "What the devil are we to do now?" "We'll have to pay for it." said Percy. "There's nothing else we can do. If we don't, we'll be had up for stealing it, and they'll probably find out about the logs as well." "So much for your cheap winter logs," snarled Charlie, and he quivered with rage as he stamped away.

"We can't get all the sacks on now," said Percy, "not without that rope." "No," said Ben, "We'll just have to load what we can, and leave the rest." "What, after we've carted them all this way, and nearly broken every bone in my body while we did it?" said Charlie. "I told you we shouldn't have taken so many, didn't I?" Ben didn't answer. He was wondering just how much new ropes cost nowadays.

Ben had lifted the first of the sacks back into the trailer when a peculiar strangled cry from Old Charlie caused him to spin round. "You stinking idiot, you!" bawled the old man, quivering again. "You know what it is that you've had us a-cartin round the countryside, don't you?" Ben looked baffled. "Look here!" sang out Charlie, dancing with rage, "Just look at this lot!"

As they had unloaded the sacks, some of them had tipped over. The bags all had logs on top of them all right, but those few logs were only a cover. Someone had used the bonfire to get rid of a large quantity of unwanted rubbish. Beneath the logs, each sack was filled with swedes. Unusable, club root infected swedes.

CHAPTER TEN.

TALLY HO!

In the quiet weeks before Christmas, when the farming activities were at their lowest, the call of the huntsman's horn could often be heard over the countryside. Landowners and farmers, together with any of the local businessmen who could afford sufficient time, would leave their mundane chores, and dressed up in coats of scarlet or black, would adopt the role of equestrian gladiators for the day, turning out to confront the fox with as much ostentation and drama as a gang of middle aged St. Georges, each going to meet their respective dragons.

Not everyone in the village was in favour of the hunt, and the customers in the Post Office were roughly equally divided between the pros and the antis. George, the landlord of the village pub, was naturally in favour of the meet, which was always held at his premises and brought him a considerable amount of business and advertisement. Clem, a young council worker, was chief spokesman against the sport, and regarded it as being as outdated as bull-baiting. "There's no excuse at all for fox hunting nowadays," he said. "There's better ways of getting rid of an animal than chasing him to death with a pack of dogs and a load of rich horsemen. You should come clean, and admit that it's a cruel way of doing things, and that you enjoy being cruel. It's just as bad as the things you blame the fox for doing, like killing a chicken when he isn't hungry. You should all be hunted yourselves for doing it, that would only be fair." "It's funny how you suddenly seem to be concerned about animals," said George. "You've never shown any kindness towards them before. I know for a fact that you've pulled the necks of hundreds of birds, usually somebody else's, and it never seemed to keep you awake at nights." "That's not the same thing," said Clem. "I'm not admitting anything, but even if you were right, it's not the same as hunting. I only kill to eat, not for the pleasure of it." "How about dogs then?" said George. "You taunt my old dog something cruel, you drive him mad every time you go past the gate. He'll have you for that one day, you see if he don't." "Oh, that dog of yours is a nasty tempered devil," said Clem. "He always makes a row, whenever he sees me, and he won't be quiet when he's told. I don't like him and he don't like me." "No, and I can't see a fox being very fond of you either," said George. "They've got a lot of sense, have foxes. Anyway, the hunt will go on as usual, and I'll bet you'll be there in the crowd to see them off, like most people." "That I won't," said Clem. "I'll be working hard, but if they should happen to pass my way, and there's a fox ahead of them, I know whose side I'll be on. If there's anything I can do to stop them getting the fox, I'll do it."

The horses stood on the pub forecourt and snorted and stamped their feet in the early morning sun, as the riders drank their stirrup cups. The crowd of villagers stood around and watched, at a respectable distance, while George, dressed in a long white apron of the style worn in the last century, brought the glasses out to the huntsmen on a large silver tray. A photographer from the local press was taking pictures of the colourful scene, or was trying to, but his subjects wouldn't keep still for a second. The pack of hounds was milling about nervously, impatient to be running, and George's dog, behind the hedge, paced back and forth and whined, realising that he was missing something exciting.

The huntsmen were a motley crew, with none of the style and grace of the shire hunts. The Master of Foxhounds, who was a local solicitor, sat astride a large black horse and fought for control, as the animal pranced sideways, taking him neatly out of shot every time a photograph was taken. A farmer's wife, her ample figure burdening a horse that looked far too small to be taking part in such grown up activities, had the opposite sort of trouble. Her mount didn't move sideways, but backed its way slowly around the forecourt, and persistently dropped its head, as if trying to slide her gently off its back and over its neck. This motion led to the lady being almost permanently in the position of having her head well down over the horses neck and her well padded posterior high in the air. As the little horse shook its head and backed around in circles, it managed to present the photographer each time round with what must have been the least flattering angle of its rider. Her farmer husband, who was an arable farmer, mainly because he was frightened of most animals, had been nagged into joining the hunt by his wife, whose main ambition it was to climb a few rungs higher up the social ladder. He had braced himself for the ordeal by taking a couple of stiff drinks before he had set off. These, on a nervous and empty stomach, didn't mix at all well with the stirrup cup, which he had gulped down greedily, his mouth being dry with fear. He swayed in the saddle, even when his horse stood quite still, and when his wandering wife backed into him on one of her rounds, he fell off, and lay petrified on his back, while a couple of large hounds licked his face. The photographer then got his first clear shot of the morning, and the farmer's fear-laden expression, as he gazed up at his wife's bulk looming backwards over him, was caught and recorded for all time.

Farmer Jackson, a local man who rarely mixed, made one of his rare public appearances, and though he managed to control his spirited young mare with expertise, he did so with no outward signs of enjoyment. This was not surprising, for he was an unusually serious type, and had recently been the subject of a good deal of ill-founded gossip, which had done nothing to dispel any of his natural gloom.

In village life, if there is any aspect of a person's affairs that is not made known to one and all, then rumours arise, and then these rumours are developed and enlarged until even a sworn statement of the truth by the person concerned will be disbelieved in favour of the rumour. So it was in our village when the man moved in as a lodger with the Jackson family.

Farmer Jackson and his wife were in their late thirties, and they had one child, a girl of sixteen. She was an exceptionally pretty girl, and was much pursued by the young men of the village. The lodger was barely twenty five years of age, and he hadn't been in his lodgings long before the gossip started. He was seen at church on Sundays with the Jackson family, and rumours soon had it that he and the Jackson girl were man and wife in all but the legal sense.

"Disgusting," was the usual comment. "How Gertrude and Farmer Jackson can allow it to go on, I just don't know. They shouldn't be allowed in church on a Sunday, living in sin like that." The vicar himself must have heard at least some of the gossip, but he never referred to it. The state of affairs continued, week after week, and the older women began eyeing the young girl's figure at church on Sundays. The opinion was often voiced that she was "puttin' a bit of weight on, filling out a bit. Only to be expected though, if you know what I mean."

The young girl's parents must have been aware of the rumours too, but they ignored them, and conducted themselves with unshakable dignity. Farmer Jackson had no worries at all where his daughter was concerned, and as it turned out later, the girl had quietly become engaged to a farmer's son who was only a couple of years older than herself, just about at the time the rumours were at their height. While the villagers were speculating about her morals, she and her boyfriend had spent most of their evenings sitting together, in the company of her parents, playing records and reading, and saving up for their future wedding.

Thus the local grapevine was proved totally wrong when the lodger left his lodgings after his stay of several weeks. It had been confidently predicted that the Jackson girl would run off with the man when he left, but she didn't. She had eyes only for her young farmer. It was Farmer Jackson's wife Gertrude who ran off with the lodger.

Farmer Jackson held his mare on a very tight rein, as he kept her almost motionless on the forecourt, and waited for the others to settle down. "Steady, Gertrude," he said to the animal, in a loud, emotionless voice. "Steady I say, steady, Gertrude." The horse obeyed, and remained comparatively still, but the roving eye and quivering limbs gave the spectators the impression that if the mare ever got the bit between her teeth, she would ignore his commands for evermore, and set off on a course of her own choice.

A lone horseman came trotting up the road, a stringy,

149

untidy figure, on a stringy, untidy horse. A quiet cheer came from the crowd as they recognised the rider, for his name was Osbert, and as he was over ninety years of age, he shouldn't have been riding at all. But Osbert couldn't be measured by the same standards that applied to the rest of the community. I had first met him when he had been a customer in the Post Office, and had been amused by the way that he kept referring to me as "Young boy," or "Young feller-me-lad." I had once remarked, casually, that I was over forty, and it wasn't often that anyone referred to me as a youngster. "Well I'm ninety, which is double your age." said Osbert. "So to me you are still a youngster. Anyway, I didn't even get married until I was forty-five, and I gave up wrestling at the same time." I tried to imagine myself wrestling, at the age of forty-five, and my hand shook as I handed him his change. "Mind you," said Osbert, "I took up the sport again, when I was forty-nine. I had time and energy to spare, you see." He gave me a serious wink. "In fact," he said, "Between you and me, there wasn't half as much to this marriage business as I'd been led to believe."

Osbert refused the offered drink, and took his place by Farmer Jackson's side, impatient to be off. The crowd watched in fascination, as the whipper-in rode up and ordered the hounds back in a group. In all the commotion no-one noticed that George's dog had found a gap in the hedge, and had squeezed his way out and joined the pack.

Across the field from the pub, Horace, one of the villages many keen gardeners, was walking round his plot, broadcasting handfuls of lime around, when he heard the sound of the hunt in the distance. "Hoick, Hoick," called the huntsmen, encouraging the hounds as they searched for a scent. The dogs circled, feathering their tails, uncertain. "Whipper-in," called the solicitor

150

to his servant, "What the deuce is wrong with those hounds? They're all at fault, they haven't had a whiff of a scent yet." "I can't understand it," said the Whipper-in. "Perhaps they've been unsettled by those curs we've picked up. There's three or four of them joined the pack. You'd think that people would keep their dogs indoors, they all know there's a hunt on." There were indeed several stray dogs in the pack, apart from George's mongrel, and they dashed around, barking and yelping, as the better trained hounds searched for a scent. The hounds covered the ground with their noses down, but George's dog held its head high, and looked around. The hair on its neck rose, as it saw something that it didn't like, over the field, and it growled deeply. A small terrier, already in a frenzy of excitement, yapped loudly as it heard the growl, and the other stray dogs also barked and ran forward. George's dog pushed its way through the hedge and set off over the field at a run towards its target. The little terrier followed, still yapping, and the strays, also still barking, went after them. One of the hounds, carried away by the pack instinct, forgot his training, and giving voice, followed. The whole pack then set off, clearing the ditch, scrambling through the hedge, and streaming out over the field.

"Tally ho," cried the solicitor. "Now they're running." "They're not running," said the Whipper-in, "they're rioting." The horses charged at the hedge, the solicitor in the lead. The farmer's wife was still having the old trouble and approached the hedge in her uncomfortable posture. When her little horse stopped dead, she rolled very slowly over its neck, and disappeared into the ditch. Her husband, who was white-faced with sheer terror now, held on for dear life as his horse, determined to be front runner, cleared the hedge with feet to spare, and thundered across the field after the hounds.

When Horace saw the dogs approaching him, he wasn't unduly alarmed. He was young, and a big man, and didn't scare easily, but it did strike him as being a little odd that this big mongrel should suddenly come racing towards him, barking and snarling like a wild thing. As the dog came closer, Horace decided that it might not be a bad idea to head for the house, if only to get some kind of weapon with which to defend himself. He moved in that direction, but the dog swerved, and headed him off. Horace picked up a clod of earth and flung it towards the approaching animal. "Get out of it," he shouted, in a voice that would have scared off most animals and many men. This dog didn't even pause, it came straight at him. Horace dodged, and prepared to stand his ground, and show this vicious dog a thing or two, when he caught sight of another dog, also racing towards him. It was a little terrier, and it was yelping hysterically. Further back, there were two or three more, all barking and running. He dodged behind his wheelbarrow. What was going on? He looked over the garden and the field once more, and then he saw the pack of hounds. His blood ran cold. They were all running towards him, giving voice as they came. Horace dropped his bag of lime, and ran. He was only a few yards ahead of the first dog, so he put on all the speed that he could muster. He couldn't get to his own front door, so he cleared the fence at one leap, and ran towards his neighbour's house. He didn't waste time knocking, but flung the door open and leapt inside. His neighbour and his wife were sitting at the kitchen table, their own little dog at their feet, when Horace burst in on them. "What the—?" said the neighbour, jumping to his feet. "Sorry about this," panted Horace, without stopping. "I'll explain later, and he was gone. He shot through the house to the front door. Behind him, the back door hadn't had time to swing to before the first dog leapt through the gap. The door swung wide, and the first dog was followed by three more. The little dog jumped up and ran round the room, yapping. The dogs streamed through the house, pushing chairs aside, while the occupants watched, speechless. Then the pack appeared, the hounds baying, their tongues lolling. Horace had fumbled with the front door for a second, and then, when he had failed to close it properly, had run towards the door of his own house. The pack poured through the house. The pack that had been only twenty in number at the start of the hunt, now had grown to nearer forty, as more and more mongrels joined in the chase. "Get out, all of you," shouted the householder, while his wife stood on a chair and screamed. The tablecloth went sliding to the floor as the pack passed by, sending the mugs and plates crashing. "Lock the door," shouted the woman to her husband, as the flood of dogs began to recede. "Put the bolt on, quickly, or we'll have the horses through next." The hounds left, still running and baying. As they went, the little dog went with them.

Horace tried his front door, and when it didn't open, recalled that he had locked it from the inside. He could hear the dogs, coming quickly. He couldn't go back to his neighbours, and he couldn't get into his own home, what could he do? He looked round desperately, and saw the church, just across the next field. The church, he thought. Sanctuary, that was the answer. He negotiated the hedge with difficulty, and with the last of his strength crossed the field, staggering as he went.

The dogs, after circling briefly around Horace's front door, set off towards the church, George's large mongrel still in the lead. A long way behind the pack, shouting and brandishing his whip, came the Whipper-in. He was closely followed by the irate solicitor, with the other hunters spaced well out behind him. Of the nervous farmer and his headstrong mount there was no sign, but

153

his wife was there on the horizon, head down and bottom up.

Horace reached the church, and dashing through the door, slammed it behind him, drawing the heavy old bolt. Then he sat panting on the floor, while outside, he heard the first of the dogs hit the door heavily. Then came the small terriers, still yapping non-stop. Then the pack arrived, all giving tongue together, and Horace's blood ran cold again at the sound. There was the sound of hooves, and the first of the horses arrived. "Holloo, Holloo," called the Whipper-in. "Hey, Major, Captain, Shandy." The dogs so named seemed to ignore the man, and they flung themselves at the door again.

It was the vicar who restored order to the churchyard. He was from a hunting and shooting family himself, but was definitely anti-hunting. His wrath mounted as he surveyed the scene, and his voice carried a strange authority when he spoke. He used his best pulpit voice, and standing tall on one of the gravestones, addressed himself to the Master of Foxhounds and the Whipper-in. "What you are guilty of comes very close to sacrilege." he said. "You debase the animals that you ride. You debase the dogs that you encourage in their savagery. You debase all mankind by surrendering to the darker side of your nature, but worst of all, you desecrate this holy place, these prayer-soaked stones, by your presence on such an ungodly errand. Begone, before the wrath of heaven falls upon you." He pointed dramatically, a towering figure, his face a mask of righteous anger. The solicitor and the Whipper-in turned and left without a word. Major, the leading hound, followed them grudgingly, and soon the whole pack streamed after him, with the mongrels and curs bringing up the rear. George's dog seemed to be extremely reluctant to leave his quarry hiding in the church, but he went also, looking back over his shoulder now and then, and growling, as he went.

The horses were returning to the village pub, from all points of the compass. Not a fox had been seen, not a scent picked up, and they were in a quiet mood as the main body of riders made their way along the road. They were met suddenly by the nervous farmer, who, appearing round a bend in the road, headed straight towards them, travelling fast. He was still trying feebly to control his high-spirited horse, which had taken him, much against his will, miles across country, and now by pure chance, was heading in the direction of the church. He passed through the group of riders at a gallop, as with staring eyes and white-knuckled grip, he tried to slow his mount. The horse paid no attention at all to his commands, knowing full well by this time who was the master, but it did realise that all the other horses were going in the opposite direction, and that he should be in front of them, not behind. The horse slid to a stop, then turned round sharply. The frightened farmer lurched in the saddle and almost fell, but before he could recover, the horse set off after the pack, and he was hanging on for his life again. He gained himself a slightly more secure position, and as his speeding steed caught up with the others, who were proceeding at a walking pace, he found enough courage to release his grip with one hand and wave the hunting crop that his wife had insisted that he should carry, for appearance. "Look out," he called pleadingly. "I can't stop." The horses parted as he approached, and he had a momentary glimpse of his wife, once more bent in her perilous position, as he passed. His wildly waving whip struck the tight expanse of jodhpurs with a loud slap as he galloped on, and she once again rolled slowly over the little horse's neck, as her husband disappeared down the lane.

That evening, Horace stood at the bar of the village pub, drinking and thinking, alone. Around him, all the other customers were talking loudly, mostly about the day's hunting. "I've never known a pack to take off after a man like that before." said Percy. "I can't for the life of me reckon out what it was that set 'em off." "It was George's dog, he started it," said Charlie. "He seemed to have a grudge against the bloke." "Well, he deserved all that he got," said Jack. "In fact, as he isn't in here at the moment, I'll let you all in on a bit of a secret. I've seen the way that Clem taunts that dog, you all have, and George has had to have a word with him more than once. That's not good enough, specially for a man that says he likes animals, and if I was as tall as some of you lot, I'd have done something about it long ago. Now I happen to have an old shirt, one that I never wear. A bright check one, just like them that Clem always has on. Well, I put this old shirt on a stick, and kept on poking it round the corner so as the dog could see it, but it couldn't see me. I got him all worked up, ready to tear that shirt to bits, then I took it away. I made sure this morning before I went to work that there was a small gap in the hedge, so as he could get through if he really wanted to. I thought I'd watch, see, next time Clem came by, wearing that shirt of his, and shouting at the dog. I didn't know that he would be watching the hunt this morning though, I thought he would be working, like me. But I could have told you what would have happened. The dog had been trained to attack that shirt, you see. I wish I'd been here to see it happen. It must have been sort of poetic justice, and I reckon I was pretty smart to work it out." He smiled round at the regulars, but no-one smiled back.

Horace put down his pint and slowly walked over to Jack. He looked down at the slight, blue denimmed figure, and then slowly began to remove his sweater, pulling it up over his head. "It never occurred to you, I suppose," he said, "that someone else might have a check shirt, just like that one." "Well, er, I've never seen anybody else wearing a shirt like that." said Jack, staring in fascination at the mass of bright check that covered Horace's chest now that the sweater was removed. "You wouldn't, would you, if the person only wore the old shirt for gardening, and jobs of that sort." said Horace, slowly rolling up his sleeves. "Er, was it you today, and not Clem?" asked Jack in a small voice. "It was," said Horace. "Clem was working. The dog never saw him, it saw me, or it saw my shirt." Jack swallowed. "Oh Law!" he said. "I've done it again." Horace flexed his muscles and cracked his knuckle joints loudly. "What are you doing?" asked Jack. "I'm training myself," said Horace, "Rather as you trained that dog. I'm training myself to catch a certain little rat." Jack looked round the bar, which was strangely silent. He saw no sign of sympathy in any of the faces, either the pro-hunt crowd, or the antis. "Oh Gaw!" he said, then turned suddenly and shot out of the door. "Hey, you come back here," shouted Horace, and set off after him. They crossed the pub forecourt, travelling at speed, and George's dog, hearing the chase, and then seeing the hated check shirt, barked with excitement, and charging through the gap in the hedge, tore off up the road after the two men, still barking furiously. Other dogs began to bark, and the various mongrels, who had enjoyed their exercises earlier in the day, answered the call and joined in the chase. The pack of dogs grew larger by the second.

The crowd of regulars stood on the forecourt of the pub and watched the strange hunt disappear in the distance. "They're heading for the church again by the look of it," said Percy. "And it's a toss up whether they get there before Horace catches up with Jack, or the dogs catch up with Horace. I wouldn't like to bet on the outcome." "It won't do Jack any good to lock himself up in there with Horace," said Charlie. "And if they do get in, they'll have a long stay. There's nobody there to call the dogs off, is there?" "I can't work out who's right and who's wrong in this caper." said Ben. "It takes a bit of fathoming." "I should leave it to the almighty." said the vicar's voice from the edge of the group. The regulars turned, the clergyman was wearing an expression of satisfaction that was hard to explain. "What do you mean, vicar?" said Ben. "What do you know that we don't?" "I know that after today's incident I decided that people were not treating the church with the respect that they should. He rattled something in his pocket, and smiled. "So, before I came away, I locked the church door."

CHAPTER ELEVEN.

GOODWILL AND ALL THAT.

It was Miss Money, in close collaboration with the schoolmistress, who arranged the children's Christmas party. She told a meeting of the Village Hall Committee that she thought that the children of our village had been somewhat neglected over the years, at least where Christmas was concerned. "They seem to think that Father Christmas lives in a big store in the city," she said. "They have to go to town to see him, and they think that he doesn't know about their village, I know that we always give them tea and cakes, but I would like to arrange for Santa to visit the school, with his sledge and all the trappings. I'd like us to organise a really spectacular Christmas party this year, within the limits of our budget, of course."

We had been selling raffle tickets in the Post Office for weeks, and so had George, at the village pub. Housewives had organised coffee mornings and jumble sales, and with so many villagers participating in the fund raising, money for the Christmas party was no problem. But the choice of a Santa Claus was.

Most of the farmers were very busy at that time of the year, the sugar beet harvest being in full swing, and as the party was to be held well before Christmas, those adult males who worked in the city were not yet on holiday. The problem was discussed over cups of tea in the village hall. After failing to provide an answer to the problem, one farmer's wife tentatively suggested that the part might be played by a woman, if the disguise was heavy enough. "I don't see why not," said one buxom female with theatrical ambitions. "After all, if the little beggars aren't supposed to know who it is under the false whiskers, it don't make any difference, do it?" Miss Money, who thought to herself that the sight of the speaker in whiskers might very well frighten the children into nightmares, pursed her lips, and let it be known that she found the idea of a transvestite Santa rather improper. Rather than stoop to that, she said, she would turn to one of the pensioners of the village, many of whom would regard a request for their services as a great compliment. The other ladies were not too sure about this, and the men of the committee, many of whom were pensioners themselves, wisely remained silent.

The ladies discussed the eligibility of the candidates, with a frankness that should have turned many an absent ear bright red. It was agreed eventually, after a great number of names had been suggested and rejected.—"He allus smells of ferrets." and "You could never hide them warts on his nose, no-how."—that the position should be offered to Ben. There were many objections to this choice, and it was a good thing that Ben was absent, as some of the remarks concerning his character were far from flattering. "We'll just have to put up with him I suppose," said the buxom one. "Not that he's got any good points at all, but he might have just a few less bad points than some of the others." Miss Money added that at least Ben was a good deal more active than many of his contemporaries, and though he had never been noted for his charitable disposition towards children, the glamour of his temporary stardom might bring out in the old man enough of the Christmas spirit to last him through the afternoon of the party. That very evening she approached Ben, and with a few flattering phrases, secured his services.

Santa was to arrive outside the school door on his sleigh, in full view of all the children, and as there was no snow yet, this presented Miss Money with her first little problem. The schoolmistress had provided a large sledge, one that had been lying unused in her garden shed, presumably awaiting the return of the ice age, for years. The sledge proved to be far too heavy to be dragged over the concrete path, and when this was attempted one evening, so many sparks were produced by the iron runners that it was thought that such an arrival would be more suitable for a demon king than a Santa Claus. The teacher came up with an idea, and two pairs of roller skates were strapped to the runners. The sledge then ran along beautifully, if somewhat too freely, it having no brakes. A small and good natured donkey had been borrowed from one of the local farmers—reindeers being rather scarce in Norfolk at the time—and in a dress rehearsal after school one evening, things didn't go too badly at all.

The little donkey only had to pull the sledge for a few yards, and appear round the corner of the school building. It did this with ease, and came to a stop obediently at the door. Ben was delighted with the performance and the two ladies greatly encouraged. "When the day comes," said the teacher. "I'll have the sledge decorated with holly and imitation snow, and the donkey will be dressed up for the occasion, to add a bit of colour." Ben was already wearing his bit of colour. He was dressed in an enormous red cloak, with matching hat and massive white whiskers and eyebrows. As he went through the rehearsal, it was noticed by the ladies that when he alighted from the sledge, his old grey working trousers and scuffed boots could be seen under his cloak. The teacher had another idea, and produced a one piece suit in bright red, made out of some very flimsy curtain material, and a pair of rubber boots that had been hand painted red to match. "Wear these on the day," she commanded. "It will add that little touch that will make all the difference." Ben looked at the costume with horror. "I can't be seen in a thing like that," he said. "Anyway, it looks too small, it'll never fit me." "But it won't show, under your cloak," soothed Miss Money, "And it won't be too tight at all, I'm sure. It was made for a very large pupil, in last year's pantomime." She didn't add that the pupil concerned had been taking the part of the devil, and that she had only just removed the tail with her nail scissors, leaving a rather jagged hole in the rear. Ben took the garment with some reluctance, but after being complimented on his performance by the two ladies, went off home in high spirits.

When the day of the party dawned, Ben was up and about very early. Although the party was not due to start until two fifteen in the afternoon, he dressed himself carefully in his bright red outfit, and then spent most of the morning sitting in front of the kitchen mirror, trying out different poses, and perfecting his benevolent smile. He hoped that someone at the party would be taking photographs, as he was sure that this was going to be a party that the children and their parents would remember for years, and they would naturally want souvenirs, and that meant pictures of Santa.

At two o'clock precisely he set off towards the school, his intention being to approach it from the rear, over the fields, so that the children wouldn't see him. His route took him past the village pub, and he paused for a moment, temptation tugging at him. A quick drink might steady his nerves and improve his performance, he thought, and he would dearly like to be seen in his full costume by some of the locals who hadn't qualified for this important role. The bar was pretty crowded, and sounds of laughter floated out on the beer laden air. The temptation was great. As he stood in thought at the side of the large Christmas tree that decorated the forecourt of the pub, two drinkers appeared in the doorway, and stood swaying as they buttoned up their coats. "Nice tree," said one man to the other. "Yes," said his friend, "But I don't care for that dummy Father Christmas much. It's all the wrong shape. It don't look lifelike at all. It's ridiculous." "Well, you'd look ridiculous if you'd been left standing about outside in all weathers," said the first man. "Maybe it's shrinking." Ben gritted his teeth. That settled it. He wasn't going in there to be insulted by every short-sighted drunk. He shrugged his shoulders aggressively, and set off, marching briskly towards the school. The two drinkers recoiled in the doorway with a gasp. "It's moving," said one. "Look at it, its little arms and legs are a-going." "Here," said the second"I'm going to get a witness to this." Ben snorted, and strode on even more quickly. As the two drinkers went back through the pub door, he crossed over the road, scrambled over the fence, and took the footpath over the field to the back of the school.

Outside the pub, George the landlord was beginning to lose his temper with the two drinkers. "I'm telling you that there ain't no Santa Claus," he said emphatically. "I ain't got one. I've never had one, and I'm never ever going to have one. Will you believe me, there ain't no Santa Claus." "But," said the customer." "But, nothing!" said George. "If you two can't hold your drinks better than this, you'd better lay off the stuff over Christmas. Santa Claus indeed, at your age!" Miss Money, passing by on her way to the school, overheard most of his remarks. "Oh, shame on you, George," she called. She wagged a white gloved finger at him. "Fancy telling them that there isn't a Santa Claus. If they believe that there is, then there is. I find it very touching that even adults can still have such beliefs." She went on her way, smiling dreamily to herself.

Santa was late, and the children were waiting. Round the corner of the building, out of sight, the donkey was hitched to the sledge. Then the heavily disguised figure of Ben squatted on board, and his sackful of presents was handed to him. After one final adjustment to his bushy beard, the bringer of gifts set forth.

Miss Money preceded him round the corner, clapping her hands and calling to the children. "Three cheers for Santa." Her voice was drowned by the babble of young voices. The classroom windows were crammed from top to bottom with small faces, and when the sledge rolled into view a roar that would have done credit to Wembley Stadium went up. Beneath his deep beard, Santa beamed. "That there donkey belongs to my uncle," piped one urchin. "Goes by the name o' Rosie." "What, you've got an uncle called Rosie?" asked a small girl. "Nar," said the boy. "I mean that the donkey's name is Rosie." "That ain't Rosie," said the girl. "Rosie ain't got silver streaks all over her." "That's just for show," said the lad. "It's like Miss Money's hat, they'll take if off later, when we ain't looking." The girl looked doubtful. "I ain't never seen Miss Money without a hat," she said. "And I don't think that is Rosie." "Well I'll show you." said the boy. "She's a good old gel, is Rosie, she always does as she's told." He strained upwards, and stuck his head sideways into the gap at the top of the window. "Whoa, Rosie." he called. Obedient as ever, the little donkey came to a stop. Behind her, the sledge kept rolling, and Santa had to stick out one red boot to act as a brake. The sledge stopped, but came to rest lightly touching the back legs of the donkey.

An ill-tempered animal would doubtless have kicked out at this unfamiliar contact, but Rosie was a gentle soul, and she didn't kick. She did, however, without any malice, lift her tail and perform that most natural of functions that makes the whole of her species so invaluable to the gardening fraternity. It was extremely unfortunate that Santa had placed his sack of gifts at the front of his sleigh, and that it was directly underneath Rosie's tail.

Miss Money was at the wrong end of the animal to actually witness the disaster, but she guessed what had happened by Rosie's demeanour and the whiff of steam. "Santa," she cried, and pointed towards the sack. Santa lunged forward and grabbed, but he was too late. The sack was now considerably fuller than it had been when he had placed it there.

"Oh Gaw, Oh Law!" said Santa. "Oh Heavens," squeaked Miss Money. "How dreadful! Whatever are we going to do?" "Help me get this lot back round the corner." said Santa. "We can't have all them little beggars watching us. They don't know what's happened. They can't see from there." Together, they turned the donkey and beat a retreat, accompanied by the boos and catcalls of the entire school. "You go back and talk to 'em," said Santa. "I'll do what I can with this stuff." He looked into his sack. "I reckon a lot of presents will have to go into the dustbin, I just hope you got plenty." "There are a lot of children away from school at the moment," said Miss Money. "There might be enough presents for those that are here." She hurried away, clicking her tongue with annoyance, to brave the impatient throng of children.

When Miss Money next appeared round the corner, Santa had placed the salvaged presents in a much smaller sack, one that he had been using to sit on in his sleigh. "Well, what do you think?" he asked. Miss Money looked at the gifts. "You've done very well." she said. "They look all right to me, and there might be enough to go round." She stopped and sniffed. "They smell absolutely awful," she said. "And so do you." Santa sat down dejectedly on the edge of his sleigh. "Well, I've done all I can." he said. "If that ain't enough, then the whole jobs off." "But we can't let the children down," said Miss Money. "Not now that they've all seen you." She thought rapidly, tapping her nose with one white gloved finger. "Wait here," she ordered, and went towards the classroom. When she reappeared, she handed Ben a small bottle. "This is a disinfectant," she said. "It's got a floral smell, and there's half a pint of it. Give your sack a good sprinkling now, and do it again from time to time. The children will no doubt unwrap their gifts as soon as they get them, and discard the wrappings, and the presents inside will be all right, they won't smell." Ben sprinkled heavily, as Miss Money tapped with impatience. "Now let's get going," she said. "Those dear little children have been kept waiting for far too long." she paused and sniffed again. "But you'd better sprinkle yourself before you go," she said. Ben did so, then placing the bottle on top of his sack of gifts, put the sack onto the sledge once more, but this time nearer to the rear.

Santa's second coming was greeted, not with cheers, as had his first, but with jeers and boos from the impatient scholars. The sleigh came to a successful stop this time, right outside the door, and Santa disembarked jauntily, and bent down to lift his sack. The waiting children had raised the windows in their impatience, and as Santa leapt from his sleigh, the hem of his twirling cloak passed temptingly close to the fingers of one of the older boys. Without taking time to think, the boy grabbed the material, and pulling several inches of it inside, slammed the window shut on it. Santa, bending towards his sack, stopped, with a peculiar sound that didn't seem to go with a cheery smile. The cloak was fastened round his neck, and the fastening grew suddenly tight. Gripping his sleigh with one hand for balance, he clawed at his throat with the other. A boy at the window, seeing his predicament, took advantage at once. "Gee up, Rosie," he called through the window, and the ever-obedient donkey obeyed. Santa stopped clawing at his throat and gripped the sleigh with both hands as it began to move away from him, sack and all. As the sleigh began to move, he appeared to increase in length before the children's eyes. His snowy white beard now contrasted beautifully with the deep crimson of his face, and his eyes, which had seemed so small and sunken only seconds ago, now seemed extremely large and liquid. The cloak, which was stretched out behind him, and his position, which was almost horizontal, gave him the appearance of flying. "Oooh, look, he's like Superman," said a small girl. "No he ain't. Not till he's stretched at least another foot," said the older boy.

Santa's neck proved to be stronger than the fastening on his cloak, much to the disappointment of the older boy. The fastening gave way, and the cloak was left trapped in the window. Santa was dragged several yards, face down, until Miss Money halted the donkey. Santa picked gravel out of his not too snowy white beard, and grumbled to Miss Money. "I can't use the cloak. It won't stay on now. Have you got a safety pin?" "Forget the cloak," ordered Miss Money. "You've got the red suit on, and the hat and beard, that will have to do." "But it don't look right," protested Santa. "The children have seen you like that already." she replied. "So what does it matter? Come on, before they begin rioting." Santa bent to pick up his sack, and the roar of laughter that came from the windows as the children caught sight of the hole where the devil's tail had been, was misinterpreted by him as renewed enthusiasm for his coming. That made him feel a lot better. Most of these children were on his side, after all. He heaved his sack onto his shoulders, and taking a deep breath and assuming his most benevolent smile, he made his entrance.

"Ho, Ho, Ho." shouted Santa, as he had so carefully rehearsed. "Ha, Ha, Ha." answered the classroom, some of them pointing and holding their sides. "You all know who I am, don't you?" asked Santa, in a voice that was meant to be full of cheer, but as his mouth was full of whiskers, the voice had just an edge of irritability to it. "Yes." chorused the children. "You're old Ben from up the road." Santa paused, astonished. How had they seen through his disguise so soon? "Well," he said, with a burst of inspiration, "I might be Ben all the rest of the year, but people can be different things at different times, now, what do you think I am today?" "My mother always says that you're a 'dirty old man," said a little blonde girl loudly, and several others voiced their agreement with this remark. Ben gritted his teeth, and the benevolent smile veered slightly towards being a savage grin. He took his seat and arranged his sack. "Now then, who's going to be first?" he said, giving the little blonde girl what he believed to be a forgiving smile. The child immediately burst into tears and ran to the teacher for safety.

"Why are you dressed up like that?" asked a small voice. "You don't look like Father Christmas at all, you look more like one of his elves." "A gnome, more like," said another voice, "Like them that they've got down at the garden centre." "Oh, he's not an elf and he's not a gnome." said an older voice, and Santa smiled towards

168

the lad. "He's just little, that's all," the boy said. "My dad reckons he's just missed being a dwarf." "He's nice," said another small girl. "I've got a doll with legs like his."

A larger than average boy came striding up to Santa, and examined him with honest curiosity and a remark-able absence of respect. He shook his head and then looked at the sack. "How about a present then?" he said, pointing. "That ain't what you're supposed to say." said Santa, perspiring now. "You're supposed to sit on my knee and tell me what you want for Christmas." "What, me? Sit on your knee?" jeered the lad. "I daren't, I might catch something." "You'll catch something in a minute all right, matey," muttered Santa through his whiskers. "Anyway," said the boy. "You're hardly any bigger than me, and you're way past your best, you probably couldn't stand my weight." The class roared and stamped their feet, and the boy, full of confidence, reached towards the sack. "Blimey," he cried, wrinkling his nose. "What a pong. What have you got in there, are you trying to gas us?" Santa stood up, as tall as he could make himself, and looked at the boy sternly from beneath his bushy eyebrows. "That smell," he said, with as much dignity as he could salvage, "Is only the smell of reindeer. They all smell like that, and you would know that, if you weren't such an ignorant little boy." "Oh, reindeer." said the boy, nodding knowingly. "You mean caribou, I suppose, or *rangifer tarandus*, that's their Latin name, you know. I've been reading about them, and you know, it's an interesting thing about caribou that—." "Never you mind about all that," said Santa sharply, and turning his back on the class, he sprinkled the sack liberally from his bottle.

He placed the bottle on top of the sack, and sat down again. "Hey, now that's useful," said the boy, and grabbed the bottle. "I'll have this instead of my present. My Mum can use it, and I bet it's worth more than any of the old rubbish that you've got in them parcels." "Give me that," snarled Santa, and he snatched the bottle from the boy and hastily stuffed it down the front of his red costume. "Now you take up a present and git orf out of it, or I'll give you a present that'll make you remember this Christmas for the rest of your blarsted life." The

170

boy looked at Ben thoughtfully for a moment, and then realising that he had gone just about as far as he could safely go, he picked up a small packet and returned to his seat.

The other children came up one by one, and collected their gifts, all except the little blonde girl, who refused point blank to go anywhere near Santa, and broke into tears whenever he happened to look her way. As the children began to open their packages, the pressure on Santa eased. He helped himself to a cup of tea, and a couple of mince pies, and began to enjoy himself once more. He stood in front of the class and watched the children at play, and his heart softened towards them. They were good kids, mainly, he told himself. He couldn't expect them all to act perfectly, after all, they had only just begun to learn about life, they hadn't got his wide experience. Forgiveness flooded through his veins. It was, after all, Christmas.

Miss Money had also noticed that the children were more settled than they had been, and appeared to be pleased with their gifts. She turned to the schoolmistress, who was fiddling with her camera, preparing to record the happy scene. "He really hasn't done too badly at all for a man of his age, has he?" she said. The teacher looked over at Santa, and drew in her breath sharply. "I think he's pretty remarkable for a man of any age." she said. "Just look at him." Miss Money looked, and turned pale as she lifted a hand to stifle a cry. Santa was standing by the teachers' table, arms akimbo. The disinfectant bottle, which he had stuck down the front of his tunic earlier, had worked its way lower during all his bending and stretching with the sack of gifts. It had come to rest somewhere below his waistband, and was now bulging through the flimsy red material in a manner that could only be described as pornographic. "Oh, my goodness," squeaked Miss Money. "If only he'd worn

171

his cloak." "Do something quickly," said the teacher. "Before any of the children notice him." "Too late for that," said Miss Money, nodding towards the older boy, who was looking at Santa with a degree of respect that had not been there earlier. The door opened, and the vicar's wife came in, with her arms laden with Christmas crackers. She smiled happily and gazed round the room, then the smile froze on her lips, and she gulped audibly as her eye fell on Ben. Ben caught her look, and gave her one of his benevolent smiles, and a wink, as any good Santa ought.

The schoolmistress took the good lady by the elbow, and whispered in her ear. "That lecherous old man is leering at you in a positively indecent manner," she said. "Try not to catch his eye, for goodness' sake. If you'd like to take those crackers through to the kitchen, I'll get rid of the old monster." The vicar's lady allowed herself to be steered away through the doorway to the kitchen, but as she went she just couldn't resist one final backward glance at the amazing bulging trousers. "Oh dear me," she said, in the safety of the kitchen. "I suppose I deserve to be turned into a pillar of salt."

It was dark by the time that Ben made his way back home. He still wore his distinctive red costume, and had indeed grown rather proud of it by this time, but had discarded the beard and the eyebrows, and the disinfectant bottle, the latter giving something of a shock to Miss Money, after he had fumbled around and then handed it back to her, and disappointment to the older boys, who had been watching him in fascination. He carried a bag of mince pies, a parting gift from the children, and as he passed the village pub on his return journey, George was just opening up for the evening trade. Ben decided that he had earned himself a pint, and reasoned that his impressive red outfit might even earn him a drink or two from interested locals.

"Gaw, what is it?" hooted George, as the diminutive red-clad figure ambled into the bar. The other customers looked at him in astonishment. "If you had a fork and a tail, you'd look just like the devil himself." said George. "What's the idea of the get-up? Are you doing it for a bet?" Ben ignored the question. "Give me a pint," he said, and stuck his hand into the bag to get himself a mince pie. He had the pie almost to his mouth when his nose told him that something was wrong. He looked at the pie with watery eyes, and then lifted the lid of it. An odour of bad eggs oozed out, and Ben recalled the smell from his own youth. "That boy!" he grated, his fists clenching. "He's put a rotten stink bomb in my mince pies." "Are you practising for something, or training for some event?" asked George, still curious. "No I'm not," snapped Ben. "I'm not training, and I'm not practising, I've just done it." He reached over for his pint, but George held on tightly to the glass and sniffed towards him. "Gaw, it smells as if you've done it all right," he said. "I'm sorry, Ben, old bor, but I can't serve you like that. I can let you have a bottle to take out if you like, but you'll have to go. It ain't fair on the others, that smell." Ben weighed the bag of mince pies in his hand for a second, as if considering whether or not to throw it at George's head, then without another word he turned and left.

The photographs were ready well before Christmas, and Miss Money made a special journey to Ben's cottage to deliver his set. She handed the pictures to him one by one, adding a little compliment with each. "This is a very good one, don't you think?" she said, and Ben took the photo. It was a very good likeness indeed, of the disrespectful scholar, who was the very last person in the world that Ben would want a picture of. The boy's expression was one of boundless mirth, and he was holding in his hand what looked to Ben like the very same paper bag that he had been presented with. He tossed the picture aside. "Where are all the pictures of me?" he demanded. "All I've seen up to now is little bits of the back of my head." "Yes," said Miss Money soothingly, "But they are very good likenesses, you must admit. It's definitely the back of your head, it couldn't very well be mistaken for anyone elses." "What are you gettin' at?" said Ben sharply. "What's so different about the back of my head?" He turned his head quickly this way and that, as if trying to see, but when his neck gave a loud crack he winced and gave up.

Ben studied the pictures once more, then brought his fist down on the table in temper. "Haven't you got any pictures with my face on?" he asked. "Not one? What the devil's wrong with me then?" "Now don't say things like that. There is one picture, and it's a very good one. I've been saving it till last," said Miss Money. "In fact it's so good that we've decided to use it on all our calendars this year. The children mount the pictures in cards, you know, and stick a little calendar underneath. We're sending one to everyone who helped with the party, and as this is the first time that we've ever had a Santa, we've decided to use your picture. You'll be seen by an awful lot of people." Ben took the picture, and looked at it doubtfully. It was a full frontal view of himself, but he was standing behind his sack of gifts, which was up on a chair, so that only his head and shoulders could be seen. The red costume showed up well; so did the snowy beard and eyebrows, but they were so bushy that hardly a feature of Ben's face could be seen beneath them. "But nobody can tell it's me under that lot." he said. "It could be anybody." "They'll all know that it's you," said Miss Money. "We'll tell them. Now cheer up. You should be very flattered." Ben grunted, and looked at the picture again, then decided to reserve his judgement.

Before Christmas came the calendars were all delivered, with a note of thanks, to all the helpers. George pinned his copy up on the wall in the bar, for all to see. Ben took to spending a good part of each evening sitting in a corner of the bar, alone, staring at his portrait. He was in this position one night when the picture caught the eye of a man standing at the bar. "Hey, have a look at this," he said to his companion. "It's that thing we saw, that time that George said that we'd had too much, and wouldn't believe us." His friend looked at the picture closely. "No," he said. "It can't be. It's meant to be a present, it's in a sack. That couldn't walk. It's one of them things like a puppet, or a doll. I'll bet it's hollow and full of chocolates or something." His friend looked even closer. "I still say it's that thing that we saw walking." he said. The other man laughed. "It couldn't I tell you." he said. "I'll bet it hasn't got any legs, that's why it's propped up in that sack, all crooked like, and look at that face. It's probably plaster, mass produced for Christmas. That would account for all them lumps and bumps." Ben scowled into his beer, and one of the men noticed him. "Here, old partner," he said. "Don't you go looking all miserable like that, sitting there by yourself. Christmas is a-coming, you know, time to enjoy yourself. Have a pint on me and cheer up." "Yes," said the second man. "Here, take this pint, I'll get another one. You know, if you don't cheer up you'll find yourself being offered the job of modelling for one of them things in that picture." The two laughed heartily, but Ben didn't join in. One man pushed the glass of beer in front of him, then raised his own. "Merry Christmas!" he said, but Ben didn't answer, or drink. "Look, old bor," said the man. "Things could be a lot worse you know, here, take a look at this." He produced a photograph, and handed it to Ben. Ben glanced at it idly, then he started. It was a picture of his enemy, the disrespectful scholar, and he was grinning, as always. "This is my boy," said the man. "He's the only one we've got, so I suppose we tend to spoil him a bit. We'd planned such a Christmas for him that you wouldn't believe, and now, right at the last minute, he's been whipped off into the hospital with his appendix. He won't be having much of a Christmas at all now, he won't be feeling like joining in the fun, and he won't even be able to eat a bit of Christmas cake. Now cheer up, and be thankful that something like that hasn't happened to you." Ben stared from the picture to the father, and then back at the picture again, and slowly a smile spread over his face. Then he slapped his thigh and chuckled. "You're right," he said, and grabbed the glass of beer with enthusiasm. "I feel better already." He beamed at the two men, and raised the glass. "Merry Christmas!" he said.

The stranger standing at the bar, and sipping his double whisky, looked at the three characters in the corner with surprise. "Merry Christmas?" he said, half to himself. "Merry? I can't see how anyone is going to be merry around here. Why there's nothing going on, nothing happening." He turned to George, as if seeking confirmation of his opinion. "Is it always like this?" he asked. "Doesn't anything ever happen around here? Is it always as dull and quiet as it is now?" George shrugged. "We like it as it is," he said. "But I suppose you're right. Nothing ever happens about this village."

THE END